1 MONTH OF
FREE
READING

at

www.ForgottenBooks.com

By purchasing this book you are eligible for one month membership to ForgottenBooks.com, giving you unlimited access to our entire collection of over 1,000,000 titles via our web site and mobile apps.

To claim your free month visit:

www.forgottenbooks.com/free806616

ISBN 978-0-267-00664-9
PIBN 10806616

STORIES

FROM

THE HARVARD ADVOCATE

BEING A COLLECTION OF
STORIES SELECTED FROM
THE ADVOCATE FROM ITS
FOUNDING, EIGHTEEN HUN-
DRED AND SIXTY-SIX, TO
THE PRESENT DAY : : : :

Harvard University
CAMBRIDGE, MASS.
ANNO M DCCC XC VI

1856

Copyright, eighteen hundred and ninety-six,

WM. B. WOLFFE.

CONTENTS.

8   CONTENTS.

PRESS OF
GRAVES & HENRY
CAMBRIDGE, MASS.
MDCCCXCVI

PREFACE.

TWO little volumes of verse, each a chronicle o a decade's history of the ADVOCATE, have already been issued. This volume, marking the thirtieth anniversary of the founding of the ADVO-CATE, appears in prose, instead of verse.

The HARVARD ADVOCATE has always tried to stand for what was best in everything pertaining to college. Its origin was due to a sure conviction that it might influence for the better many features of University life. Its attitude, as shown in the first numbers, gave it at once a position of power in educational and social improvement in the University.

Some stories of the early years are written by men who have already achieved enviable reputations in the world of literature. Other stories, more recent productions, prophesy the rising power of a later generation.

CAMBRIDGE, MASS., May 11, 1896.

THIS COPY IS NO. 1

MEMORABILIA.

MEMORABILIA.

(TRANSLATION.)

SOCRATES. Good morning, Glaucon.

GLAUCON. Good morning, O Socrates!

SOCRATES. Tell me now, Glaucon, are you just from the temple?

GLAUCON (*who has seen Socrates before*). I should say so.

SOCRATES. Whether is the business there worship, or to see if any of the young men be absent?

GLAUCON. Give it up.

SOCRATES. Is it not right that all men should be eager to learn?

GLAUCON. Most certainly, O Socrates!

SOCRATES. Are you not, then, a man?

GLAUCON (*who has seen the Sphinx*). You bet.

SOCRATES. It is plain, then, that you wish to listen to me.

GLAUCON (*somewhat mixed*). It must be so.

SOCRATES. Tell me, then, if you were to go into the Agora, and there see many citizens noting and discussing the affairs of the city, and only two or three were selling figs, would you not say that the object of the meeting was politics, and not fig peddling?

GLAUCON. Most assuredly. If I should deny it, I should be very foolish.

SOCRATES. And if there should be a crowd around me, some time in the Peireus, listening to my wise words, if, perchance, they might learn something, and two only should be matching obuli, of what would you say the crowd was composed? Ahem!

GLAUCON.   Of your disciples, certainly, O most wise Socrates.

SOCRATES.   Tell me, then, Glaucon, in the temple this morning how many were engaged in worship?

GLAUCON.   One, indeed.

SOCRATES.   Whether was one conducting the worship and many listening, or do you say that no one was listening?

GLAUCON.   Not one, in truth, save by accident.

SOCRATES.   And were there any who were busy marking the young men if they were absent?

GLAUCON.   You will find no one to deny it.

SOCRATES.   How many, then, were there?

GLAUCON.   Four, O reverend sage!

SOCRATES.   Then it seems that four were busy about the affairs of men, and one only about those things which concern the gods.

GLAUCON.   Thus it certainly was.

SOCRATES.   Do you not, then, say that in the temple, as in the Agora and in the Peireus, that the matter about which most were busy was the business of the meeting, and not that about which the few?

GLAUCON.   I do, indeed, by Jupiter! and, to-morrow morning, I will go to roll-call, and not to prayers.   Come and breakfast with me, Socrates.

C. S. Gage, '67.

THE EDITOR'S STORY.

I AM an Editor of THE ADVOCATE. I do Atoms, and one-column "Locals," with occasional Boating notices; but never — no, never, upon my honor,— Ball reports. My strongest point is in Freshman subscriptions. In these I have a most winning way, and am considered invaluable. There may have been a time when I was conceited as to my literary abilities. Let me think. Yes; I acknowledge there was. In those delightful days, when parietal persecution had compelled us to take refuge in the editorial sanctum of *The* ———— no matter what: suffice it that they lent us quills, scissors, paste-pot, and ideas, for a fortnight. In return for which we are eternally grateful, and shall never forget the time when their easy-chair was our easy-chair, and their devil our devil. In those days, I say, beside the thrilling joy of expected martyrdom, another enchanting emotion welled up in my bosom. I see, as I look upon it, that it arose in the notion that I could "sling ink." But that conceit is soon taken out of one. I had only to listen in silent agony for two or three numbers to the comments of unconscious neighbors at meal-time on my carefully elaborated masterpieces, to arrive at a fair estimate of my own abilities. Nor is this my only virtue. I dare affirm that I love my fellow-man, and reverence my fellow-woman; that I have a due respect for College-officers, and no fanatical longing to turn my Alma Mater's household topsy-turvy. Why, then, am I afflicted with this social plague-spot, this ineradicable taint? I must unburden, or it will corrupt my whole being.

But, to begin at the beginning, "I was not always thus." It was not long ago that I exulted, absolutely exulted, in the dignity of my office. I was infatuated enough to deluge my friends far and near with copies of THE ADVOCATE. A becoming blush tinged my cheek when favorable allusions were made to that paper in my presence. I even carried it with me on my visits to Dulcinea, who lives in — well, let us say, Brighton. And Dulcinea was pleased to say that some of the articles were very witty, and asked — oh! with such a glance from her lustrous eyes — which of the love sonnets were mine. Then how passionately I wished for the gift of poesy! but I dexterously avoided a direct reply. This was a time of unalloyed Arcadian bliss. Then came a blow, a cruel blow. Muffins, friend of my bosom, deserted me. His play in the field had been severely criticised by our Base-Ball reporter; and the brute insisted on wreaking sole vengeance on me, innocent. I expostulated. I assured the "dear fellow" that it was all a mistake. I promised that, at the very next match, his fielding should be lauded to the skies. In vain. What was done could not be undone; and the inexorable Muffins is friend of my bosom and confidant of my life secrets no more. Soon other desertions. Many of my schoolmates went to Yale. To these, in the first pride of exultant editorship, I had despatched THE ADVOCATE. In some obscure corner our Cynical Editor had inserted a slur on Yale. Back came letters filled with the most vituperative upbraidings; and I no longer receive urgent invitations to Thanksgiving Jubilees and Wooden Spoon Saturnalia. Again, my instructor in Ethnology had always treated me with marked condescension. I felt certain of a high average in that study. Somehow it reached the venerable man's ears that I was an Editor of that revolutionary sheet, THE ADVOCATE. What was the result? Two days' running I can stand, but not six. I defy any man to be called up six times running, and come out unscathed. He "bowled" me, and my high rank was lost. I could recount other instances of alienation equally painful; but these straws are enough to indicate the popular current. Friends and enemies alike took up the cry, "*Frenum habet in cornu*," and the world looked coldly on me.

But I had one solace. Brighton was left me. I redoubled my visits to that charming locality; and, beyond the Charles, I heeded not, nay, exulted in, the scorn of man. The more agonizing the sequel; but I must not anticipate. It was a dull, lowering day when I paid my last visit to Brighton. Was there no inward sinking of the heart, responsive to the gloom without, and ominous of coming misery? Yes, there was. The ruffled surface of the wayside mud-puddles tortured by wintry winds, the plaintive bleat of lambkins in the neighboring withered pastures, the sullen creak of the whirligig as it bore round and round its hangings of family linen in the adjacent back-yard, and the insulting leer of the younger brother as he admitted me within the portal, are all indelibly impressed upon my memory as mournful harbingers of woe. But I cannot, no,

I cannot, bring myself to enter into the details of that cruel reception. The wound is yet too raw. I had as usual, upon my previous visit, brought with me THE ADVOCATE. Some critical carper had discovered that that paper had spoken slightingly of the young ladies of Cambridge. Were not the young ladies of Brighton sisters, as it were, of the young ladies of Cambridge, and bound to resent such outrage? I was dismissed forever from the house.

And now, as the final drop in my cup of gall, my father writes that my abandoned course as an Editor of THE ADVOCATE, in recklessly attacking existing institutions and sacred ties, is bringing down his gray hairs in sorrow to the grave. Words fail me to express my misery and desolation. Was ever man so accursed before? Behold me an outcast from the social pale, a Pariah among my fellows.

E. W. Fox, '67.

GRIFFIDUS MANN.

I HEARD him coming, and waited. "You needn't look that way," he began, as he opened the door: "I know I'm a bore, but it's not polite in you to tell me of it. Yes, you did, just as plainly as though you'd said it. However, we'll not quarrel about that." He settled himself in the window-seat.

"You think you know what's coming; but you don't. It's not Memorial,— I've got tired of that; no, nor the niggardliness of the Faculty, or Corporation, or somebody, in the matter of holiday recesses. It's John." (John is his chum.)

"You're astonished? I expected you would be: that's what I came in here for. You think that because John is popular and good-natured, and, above all, a fellow of taste, it must be a privilege to live with him. I don't. As for taste, if taste means making a college room look as unlike a college room as is possible, then I admit that John has taste; but taste, then, is not a comfortable thing. When I came here, I was told that the high-toned, 'blooded' man usually had shingles hung in his room. So I joined all the societies that it didn't cost over five dollars to get into, and had the shingles neatly framed; but now John declares that shingles are a barbarity; and, as John bosses me, the shingles have been tucked away in my bedroom, where they awe no one but the goody and a few other privileged friends.

"Then the curtains. To be sure, they were more damaging to my pocket than to my feelings. I had intended to have them of Turkey red. They are common, of course; but why shouldn't they be? They certainly do give a room a warm look; and we have little enough warmth here, everyone knows. Accordingly, when curtains came up for discussion, I suggested Turkey red; but no; they weren't æsthetic (John pronounces it *ai*sthetic); and, as crash towelling was æsthetic, and produced the effect of India crape, we bought crash towelling. I never knew before that towels cost so much. I suppose it's a result of protection.

"The pictures, too, to say nothing of the frames. I had a few photographs, which I thought would do; but they were all put in the bedroom, and the walls are covered with a lot of brown things that look like pale ink-spots a little way off, and are nothing near to. But I believe that they are copies of some ancient Egyptian statues, and very interesting and beautiful. John and his friends say so, and they know. But I don't complain. Only it's very disagreeable. Say, does lunacy ever reappear in a family after a long interval? Some ancestor of mine, I believe, spent his life in a mad-house, and my great-aunt, I know, used to be very loony. I wonder — "

Just then he sneezed. "That's right," he said, very calmly; "let me sit by the window till I catch cold, so that I sha'n't trouble you any more. I shall go into a decline now, probably. Don't know but what it would be the best thing for me."

He went out. I couldn't ask him to stop longer; for I'm afraid he was right. I'm afraid I do think him a bore.

Edward Hale, '79.

JANUARY 30. The work still goes on, and every day the practised eye can detect traces of eventual improvement. Individual faults, however, are still manifest; and No. 4, in particular, has a most awkward habit of wagging his left ear on the recover. This is a vicious trick which would undoubtedly cause disturbance in the boat; and unless he can correct it before the river opens, the ear must be sacrificed.

No. 6 has lately appeared to find great difficulty in keeping his eyes in the boat, and has been subjected to severe discipline on that account. It seems that the poor man has been cruelly misjudged; for, being cross-eyed, he is obliged, in order to see the man in front of him, to keep his head at such an angle as to give a looker-on the impression that he is studying the architecture of the boat-house roof. Such is not the case.

The run was unusually lively, the crew being chased for seven miles by a policeman, who labored under the mistaken idea that the Somerville Asylum had broken loose.

JANUARY 31. All down but nine, who were in attendance upon Moody and Sankey, and, being unable to be present, sent around their cards by a small boy. If this thing occurs again, the tabernacle shall be closed! The other five men went at it with great vehemence, and did good work. No. 4's ear was tied down, and the consequent improvement in his form was very noticeable. No. 2 still "buckets" disgracefully, and is inclined to "pall" on the last three hundred strokes. The run was remarkably exhilarating. No. 6, while looking at a young lady across the street, ran into a lamp-post and was completely upset. The gas company was notified, and No. 6 will be more careful in future. He seems willing to work, and is anxious to be on the crew; but he was "raised a pet," and, being inured to luxury from early youth, allowances have to be made for him.

FEBRUARY 1. Thirteen men present, which being an unlucky number, we were obliged to diminish it by one. The coach signified his desire that some one should volunteer to sacrifice his personal pleasure to the general good by refraining from work, and immediately twelve men stepped forward with the utmost alacrity. This exhibition of unanimous self-abnegation was extremely gratifying to the coach, who thinks it conclusive evidence of a high state of discipline.

Pulled twelve strokes, which gave an average of one hundred apiece. Then ran, with the exception of No. 8, who will not be permitted to take out-door exercise with the rest of the crew until a radical change takes place in his views regarding the propriety of appearing on the streets in a pajamah and cashmere skull-cap.

E. S. Martin, '79·

FOOT-BALL AT OTHER COLLEGES.

THE foot-ball season has now fairly opened, and it is well to take a glance at what our rivals are doing. Yale has lost Thompson, who has twice turned the scale against us; but otherwise her team will probably be much the same as last year's, and there is plenty of good material with which to fill the vacancies. Captain Camp has already begun to put his men into regular training, running them in the gymnasium. Thirty men have been pledged to play against the team every afternoon, and games will probably be played with both Amherst and Trinity; so that there will be no danger of her men suffering from lack of practice. At present it hardly seems as if the team would be as good as last year's, but their playing is improving every day, and nothing but very hard work will enable our men to win the victory.

Princeton undoubtedly will have a good team, although the lower classes do not seem to possess very good material from which to choose; but it must be remembered that in Princeton, where there is no crew, all the best men go out on the foot-ball field, and work with a faithfulness not very common at Harvard.

At Cornell there has been some talk of organizing a team, but it is doubtful if it can be done this year. What Columbia will do, it is difficult to say. On the whole, the prospect should be by no means discouraging to us. We certainly have good teams to fight against; but there is plenty of excellent material in College, and our captain deserves most hearty praise, whatever be the result, for the pains he has taken, not only in keeping the men at work on the field, but in running them on the track every afternoon. What is most necessary is that every man should realize the necessity of faithful and honest work, every afternoon. Last year, we had good individual players, but they did not work together nearly as well as the Princeton team, and were not in as good condition as the Yale men. The foot-ball season is short; and while it does last, the men ought to work faithfully, if they expect to win back for Harvard the position she held three years ago.

Theodore Roosevelt, '80·

TERRIBLE CRIME IN BOSTON.

[Special Despatch to the Advocate from the H–r–ld Office.]

UNPRECEDENTED ATTACK UPON AN OFFICER BY THIRTY RUFFIANS! THE OFFICER OUTRAGEOUSLY ABUSED! THE BRAVE MAN WHIPS TWENTY-NINE OF THE VILLAINS, AND PUTS THE REST TO FLIGHT! THE Φ. B. K. SECRET EXPOSED!

H–R–LD OFFICE, 9 A. M.   Shortly after midnight on Thursday a villainous outrage occurred in our usually quiet city, which, for coolness of plot and the desperate character of its purpose, is unequalled in the annals of crime.   The perpetrators of this affair are a party of well-known ruffians who have been lurking around the lowest haunts of Old Cambridge, and whom the police have been watching with suspicion for some time.   The better to conceal their evil enterprises (this is by no means their first offence), they have been organized into a sort of club, calling themselves the Φ. B. K. (which symbols are supposed to represent the motto of the gang), and they have been careful to admit to their secret council none but those who could be safely bound to them by well-established records of crime.

It seems that on Thursday they had got wind that a certain well-known and highly-respected officer would be walking alone in an unfrequented part of our city, and they deliberately set about planning the most villainous scheme that devils' brains seem capable of devising.   At an early hour in the evening, they assembled secretly at a tavern

in a retired street of Boston, where they had
ordered a supper, to avert suspicion; and it is
supposed that there the final steps were taken
toward the completion of their infernal plot. The
landlord, whom our reporter interviewed at an
early hour this morning, says that when the party
left the tavern they were all in such a beastly state
of intoxication that not one could stir from under
the table. Be this as it may, it is certain that they
remained at the tavern drinking lemonade till the
streets were pretty well cleared of people, and the
beautiful moon had hidden her face for very dread
behind thick clouds. Then they stole forth to exe-
cute their horrible plan. Passing through C—rt
street, they proceeded stealthily down to C—m-
br–dg– street, and then passed rapidly down over
the hill. But, as they drew near their destination,
the evil spirit within them could no longer be kept
quiet, and they broke out into the vilest oaths and
threats that the oldest *H–r–ld* reporter ever has
heard, and some of them chanted a devilish war-song.
The brave officer, who had been standing a little
back from the pavement, saying his evening prayers,
and who is ever zealous to use peaceful measures,
as he heard the ruffians coming threw away his
club and pistol, and, turning his back to the mob,
as if further to conciliate them, besought them, in
the name of the Commonwealth and of the city, not
to create any disturbance. (This is testified to by
an eye-witness.) His speech is said to have lasted
fifteen minutes. At any rate, for some time he
kept back the infuriated mob by the pathos of his
appeal. But it was only the lull that precedes the

storm. Prayers could not touch those hardened hearts; and presently the captain of the gang, recovering himself, called upon his murderous followers "to find out the officer's number"; and some of the more violent villains swore brutal oaths at him, saying, "You're only a cop!" "You're only a cop!" Seeing that several of the mob were armed with cannon and kegs of nitro-glycerine, the noble officer was compelled to use force; and, notwithstanding the fact that he was alone and surrounded, with his fists he beat down the leaders of the party. He killed seven of the thirty murderers, and seriously injured twenty-two. The rest fled in fright. The injuries which the brave fellow received from battle-axes and spears and bludgeons have driven him to his couch. That such a party of desperadoes could have prowled about so long, shows the dreadful condition of our city government; and all good citizens ought to unite in giving to the suffering hero some substantial evidence (we suggest the governorship of the State) of the gratitude which they owe to him.

7.30 A. M. The noble officer is still confined to his bed. It is said that the escaped desperado intends to offer the most violent resistance to arrest, and it is feared that more bloodshed will be the result. The authorities ought to stop at no halfway measures, and let the State militia be called out, and all other active measures be taken to wipe out of existence this infernal Φ. B. K. and its supporters.

J. L. Pennypacker, '80.

NEVER went to Class Day, Nellie? Why, **you** don't know what you've missed. See here, what I got yesterday. All these envelopes, every one of them postmarked " Cambridge Sta." I don't know what that means, I'm sure. ' Stables,' I guess, for my cousin Sam said when he was in college that most all of the students had horses,— nice little ponies, you know. But you can't guess what's in these envelopes. What? Invitations? Why, you bright girl, you guessed right. They are, sure enough, invitations to Class Day. There are one, two, three, four, all alike,—those are to the Hasty Pudding—what do you call it; spread! I wish they wouldn't call it such a horrid name. Sounds like a bed-quilt. Then there are these three different ones, private spreads, you know, real swell affairs; oh, it's awfully fun; you see ever so many elegant looking fellows. But I don't believe I shall go. Why not? Oh, I don't care much about such things. Oh, you needn't laugh, Nellie. Besides, I haven't anything to wear. I've spent every cent of my allowance; and I must have something becoming. I have to wear just the right things, you know. Then I don't think I'm a very popular girl. Most all these invitations are just some kind of duty. There's that from Mr. Quits,— that man we saw at Mt. Desert, that I thought was smitten with — no, not me.—yourself, you sly girl! Why didn't he invite you to Class Day, then? I don't know; I suppose you never asked him to call on you. You don't manage your cards right, Nellie. Then this one's from that Mr. Slague,— well, I don't know, but I heard Tom Van Isher call him,— well, something not very nice. I'm sure he doesn't like him. Well, what are you laughing at now, Miss? You think I'd go if Mr. Van Isher asked me? I'd like to know what put that into your head. He hasn't asked me, anyway, and he said he was going to have a spread. Disappointed? No! Why should I be? And I'm not blushing, either, Nellie! Then I had enough of Class Day last year. You just go and stay round there, and get sick on spreads, and dance a little over in that great dining-room,— crumbs and things, I suppose, all over the floor; and get your dress all spoiled. It's perfectly ridiculous, Nellie, the dresses some girls wear out there—all in the dust and mud. You thought I said I must have a new dress? Well, one can't go in a wrapper, can they? Oh, Class Day's well enough for little, young girls, but I — who's that, the postman? Letter for me?— thank you, Mary. What is it, I wonder: "Mr. Thomas Van Isher desires the pleasure of your company on Class Day, June —." Just see, Nellie, isn't it quite too lovely? Come to think of it, I did promise to go out to his spread, and it wouldn't be polite not to, would it? I'll make papa get me that dress. I guess I am quite a popular girl. I should think you'd want to go, awfully, Nellie.

J. McG. Foster.

CONFESSIONS OF A FRIVOLOUS YOUTH.

MY name is Fitzalbatros Van Ambrosial, and I may as well say in the beginning that I am the ta-ta thing and a howling swell. I spent my early years abroad, which accounts for my slightly English accent, and this accent I have endeavored not to lose.

I live on Beacon street (our family has always lived on Beacon street), and I was an unmatriculated student in Harvard College for one year. I call myself a graduate, but the examinations were such a bore that I left after the first year. This is all introductory, however, and my object is only to tell of my society days.

I remember my first winter, and can even recall my début at Mrs. Mike McCarty's. I was really excellently dressed, for I had a new dress coat from England, of a fine diagonal, and a crush hat to match. My stockings, a mere suspicion of which appeared above my faultless pumps, were very much admired by my mother, as she looked at me after I was attired for the party. I wore my left-hand glove, and carried the other crushed in my hat rim. These details I mention, not because of their importance, but to show the care with which I had equipped myself; for this care, I believe, was the cause of my success in Boston society.

"Good-by, Fitzy," cried my father. "Don't dance too much," echoed my mother. "You look too handsome," added my maiden aunt.

I do not dance.

As I went up the stairs at Mrs. Mike McCarty's, I stepped on two or three languid beauties; but my face appearing out of my ulster, they only smiled sweetly at me, and I heard them say, "What a swell! Who is he?" I naturally felt a degree of pride, tempered by pity for the poor dear things.

After smoking a cigarette to calm my nerves, and giving a final brush to my hair, which was parted behind, I descended to the whirling scene below. It was more than I had anticipated. After speaking to my hostess, I put my one eye-glass to my eye, and timidly proceeded to gaze about me.

There were some ravishingly pretty girls in the room, and I determined to be introduced. One, Miss Tandemdogcart, was, I saw, covered with confusion on seeing me approach.

I hesitatingly said on bowing, "What liquid eyes you have!" (A rather clever introductory speech, thought I.)

"Oh! you base flatterer!" she replied.

"Not at all," I rejoined.

"I know you are," she continued.

"When I look into their dreamy depths I must speak," I ventured further.

"You make me distrust you when you speak thus," she added.

"Pray do not," I murmured.

"Well, perhaps, if you will promise not to say any more such foolish things," she whispered.

"It's very warm," I lisped, bending over her and looking fondly into her eyes.

"Yes," she faltered.

"See you later," I uttered, as I left. I made a great impression as I walked across the room.

My aunt, Mrs. Chuck-Woodchuck, thereupon dragged me up to a plain-looking girl named Miss Tank, who was very blunt and outspoken in her manner. She said as I bowed, "Are you a materialist or an idealist?"

"Yes, rather," I replied.

"I'm so glad," she rejoined.

"Aw, too much pleasure, I assure you," I continued.

"Don't you think Daisy Miller is too overdrawn to be the typical representation of the best æsthetic production of Boston culture, or do you prefer the ideas of Joseph Cook?" she ventured further.

"Yes, James is quite too awfully clever; yes, indeed," I added.

"Do you attend the Summer School of Philosophy at Concord?" she murmured confidingly.

"No, not today; no," I stuttered, getting a little flurried.

"Oh! I see you are one of those interesting atheists," she continued.

"Yes, I will get you some," I uttered, as I slid away.

Later in the evening I sat with Miss Tank and looked over some beautiful drawings taken from the *Harvard Lampoon*. She talked much and in an interesting manner. I thought I knew what she meant by the obscuro, but did not understand the chiascuro.

After this party came dinners and calls and lunches for two seasons. I might also give you many pages of my diary, but will spare you.   Then I flirted with Miss Tandemdogcart, but really liked Miss Tank better, and saw a great deal of her the next winter; indeed, I married her, and we have now a little boy.   I have settled down, really.

RAC.

Carleton Sprague, '81.

STORIES FOR THE YOUNG.

(Each story intended to teach some valuable moral lesson.)

I. JOHNNY KLEENER, THE THOUGHTFUL NEWSBOY.

IT was late in the afternoon, and the streets were filled with people hurrying homeward from their work. In and out through the throng of people slipped little Johnny Kleener, our hero, or, rather, our illustrative example. Every now and then he glanced with a smile of satisfaction to the very small bundle of papers under his arm, for only two *Stars* and a *Globe* were left on his hands. He wasn't the kind of a boy to get "stuck" on papers; not he. No boy in Boston had more salable news than Johnny. When there was anything fresh and startling, well and good; when there wasn't anything, he understood his duty to the public, and supplied the deficiency. One might have seen at a glance that he was a "smart" boy; and, moreover, that he was a thoughtful boy. There lay the secret of his great success. For example, most newsboys, as we all know, are the sole supports of widowed mothers, but Johnny wasn't. He let "the old woam," as he affectionately termed her, trudge over to the city soup-house, or "diet kitchen," for most of her sustenance. Johnny said the exercise did her good. Here, in so slight a matter as his mother's health, we see evidences of the boy's care.

Now, on this particular afternoon, although only a few papers were left, he set his inventive faculty to work, and began to cry out very attractive news.

There was nothing mean about him; he gave just as choice an assortment of news to sell a *Star* as to sell an *Advertiser*. He hadn't long to wait for his reward; for very soon a man rushed up to him in a tremendous hurry.

"Here, boy!" he called; "give me a *Herald*,— quick." Johnny handed out a *Globe*, title-page down.

The man tossed a bright two-cent piece to the boy and was off. Johnny caught the coin, looked at it sharply, pocketed it, and was off, too,— in the other direction. The coin was a five-dollar gold piece. Now, no one must think that Johnny meant to keep this money, for he didn't. .He meant to spend it; and he hastened to invest a small fraction of it in a box at the Opera House.* Can you imagine the poor lad's righteous indignation when he presented that miserable, cheating coin at the box-office, and was told that it was counterfeit? Perhaps he said, "Darn the ole thing,"— perhaps he said something else. However that may be, the thoughtful boy did not throw the "ole thing" away; and when that night he entered "2 sents to Profit & Loss," he made a "?" against the item, as though the end was not yet.

  *   *   *   *   *   *   *   *

A week or so afterwards, while Johnny was selling his papers on Washington street, a jolly-looking old gentleman came towards him.

"Give me a *Herald*, my little fellow," said he; "and here — Bless me, where are my glasses? Never mind; that is a two-cent piece, I think."

*Gray's Opera House.

Truth "stranger than fiction" compels me to say that for the second time Johnny received a five-dollar gold piece for two cents.* He put it away quickly, and hastened — at a safe distance — after the old gentleman, who jogged along down State street to his office. Johnny was very, very thoughtful all day long. In the afternoon, when the twilight was making all things dim, when it was too dark to see plainly and too light to use the gas, he tapped on the door of the merchant's office.

"Come in," said the old gentleman. "What do you wish, my boy?"

"Please, sir," said Johnny, putting on his choicest moral expression — his *Sunday Herald* expression — "Please, sir, you gave me a gold piece this morning by mistake, and — and"— here came a sob — "although we're very po—o—r, sir, I couldn't keep it, and so I brought it to you."

"Bless my heart," said the old merchant. "Well, well; you are an honest boy. It was an old pocket piece of mine, too. Let's see. I haven't much change about me, but here's a couple of dollars for you, my boy; and if you'll call in the morning, perhaps I may give you something better."

Johnny thanked him, wishing inwardly for "something better" then and there. Yet he was fairly well content with the day's work, and hurried off, thinking how much he should enjoy the six dollars and ninety-eight cents that had rewarded his financial efforts, for the thoughtful boy had given the old gentleman the counterfeit coin.

---

*This may seem a trifle improbable, but the fact is necessary to the story — it is a case of moral lie cents.

AUTHOR'S NOTE.—In the above story, I have tried to illustrate the advantages of a thoughtful character. In devoting myself to that object, I may possibly have left the illustrative example deficient in a few desirable qualities. This, I hope to remedy by continuing the series until each virtue has been made the subject of a story. By reading *all* of these stories, it is plain that a very high ideal may be formed. One word of caution I may add for the young reader: However great was Johnny's success, remember that, for most people, " it is better to give counterfeit money than to receive it."

C. R. Clapp, '84.

WHY SPARTACUS LOST THE PRIZE.

A FEW weeks ago, while reclining one evening
in my easy-chair, I became painfully aware
that the man who roomed above me was practising
a speech, for at frequent intervals he would run
across the floor and stamp most violently, whereupon large and small pieces of plaster from the
ceiling would fall about me. Night after night the
speech was rehearsed with constantly increasing
effects. I could neither study, read, nor sleep.

At last, in sheer desperation, I determined to try
myself for one of the prizes; not that I have any
ability in speaking, for I am quite aware that such
is not the case, and, more than this, I stutter terribly; but it seemed to me that I could perhaps
neutralize the declamatory demonstrations of my
neighbor if I should indulge in a little elocution of
my own. I could also have an excuse for stamping
upon the floor, and for showering down pieces of
plaster upon the head of the unfortunate man in
the room below. He was a " subscription fiend,"
and the bare thoughts of being able to bury him
in plaster debris, perhaps put out his eyes, were
enough to make me decide.

I chose " Spartacus to the Gladiators," a really
excellent piece for action, and began at once to re-
hearse it. I roared, rushed about, and, where the
sense seemed to require it, stamped. It is true
that I struggled in the midst of difficulties, for sometimes I could scarcely hear myself by reason of
the noise caused by dumb-bells, base-ball bats, and

pieces of kindling wood, which were hurled against my door by my unappreciative neighbors.

At last, one night, the door flew from its hinges, and before my astonished gaze stood the subscription man, the proctor, the janitor, and several students.

"Ye call me ch–ch–ch–ch–chief, and ye der–der–der–do wer–wer–wer–well to call him ch–ch–ch–chief —"

"See here," screamed the janitor, "do you know that you are in a fair way to demolish the entire building, to say nothing of driving mad some dozen or more students?"

"If there ber–ber–ber–be one among yer–yer–yer–you who–who–who let him st–st–st–st–step fer–fer–forth — st–st–st–step forth."

At this the proctor, who was always a valiant man, considering his large build, with the help of six students, undertook to suppress any further declamation; and succeeded, after knocking me down, in convincing me that Spartacus would never take a prize.

One of my assailants kindly suggested that I had better eschew tragedy and try something in the poetic line.

"Spooks, old boy, a poem would suit your voice first rate. Try 'The boy stood on the burning deck.' You've got just the physique for such a piece as that."

Of course several days were lost in looking up a new piece, but I finally chose " Barbara Frietchie," inasmuch as I had learned from reliable sources that it was a popular piece with the judges.

One verse of this poem bothered me a great deal,—

> " Halt! the dust-brown ranks stood fast,
> Fire ! out blazed the rifle blast."

It did seem as though I could never get that word " fire " out of my mouth, but when it did come, it came with a vengeance,—" fer–fer–fer–fer–fer–fer– FIRE."

I tried this word over and over again until I found I could shout it out without the least hesitation.

I had just begun to repeat it from the beginning, " Up fr–fr–fr–from the me–me–me–meadows rich with ker–ker–ker–corn, cle–cler— " when a ladder was suddenly thrust through my window, and a fireman's head appeared.

" Hullo there ! Wha–wha–wha–wha–what's ther– ther–ther–ther–the — "

Before I could inquire further I was lifted off my feet and dashed against the wall by a stream of water from a four-inch pipe.

The room became quickly crowded with firemen, students, and " muckers," who began immediately to throw all my furniture and bric-a-brac out of the window. When everything had been thus satisfactorily and summarily disposed of, they very naturally began to look for the fire.

Wiping the water from my face and eyes I tried to tell them that there was no " fer–fer–fer–fer–fire."

As soon as it dawned across their minds that it was a false alarm, they began to swear in a most approved fashion, and I am led to believe from the language used on this occasion, and from the heartless way in which they kicked me about for giving the alarm, that they will experience not the slightest difficulty in finding all the fire they want hereafter, "In that be–be–be–bourne from wher–wher–wher–whence no traveller returns."

W. E. C. Smith, '83·

AN ARTIST'S STORY.

AS I was tramping along a dusty road in North Conway, one day last summer, I saw just ahead a small, middle-aged man carrying a camp-stool, a large white umbrella, and a package that, judging from the brilliant spots of color on the outside, contained paint. Now, being something of an art amateur, I felt interested; and quickening my pace, soon caught up with him.

"On a sketching trip?" said I.

"No," said he; "not exactly. I gen'rally do finished work myself. I leave scrawly, sketchy letterin' an' fence-daubin' to cheap hands; an' keep myself to do the fancy figgers an' varygated printin' on the big rocks."

"Then," said I slowly, "you are an — an artist?"

"Why, cert'nly I am," answered he. "The Egyptian Hair Renewer keeps me to illustrate the wonderful results of usin' that preparation. Every time I see a good flat rock or ledge, I beautify that same rock with the picture of a lovely female with red hair floatin' down to her heels; we used to do the hair in black, but brick red is gettin' to be more fash'nable."

My first impulse was to drown the man in his own paint; but he seemed to take such an honest pride in his work, that I couldn't even bear to hint that he was a public nuisance and that he ought to be prosecuted. As we walked sociably along, he began to talk about his trade, or, as he termed it, "his profession."

"Oh," said he, "there are a few of us that are at the top, but we all get a set-back now an' then. I came to North Conway for the first time last May; an' as soon as I spotted these ledges, says I, 'There's your place for a swell display.' It is, you know, a wall of rock two hundred feet high, an' not a foot-hold on it. On the other side there is a roundabout path, long, steep, an' hard to climb; but I went up one day, walked all over the hill, an' at last found jest the place. It was almost at the highest pint of the ledge, an' down below, about twenty foot, jutted out a little shelf p'raps three foot wide. 'Now,' says I, 'this advertisement must be worthy of the place; an' the only thing to suit the sublimeness of this spot is po'try,— the twin sister of my own art.' I laid awake all that night an' composed; an' the next day had this little poem ready:

> "'O stranger, when your locks get fewer,
>   And when thereby you've been appalled,
>   Buy the Egyptian Hair Renewer,
>   And to its use become enthralled.'

"Now, sir, that was the proudest moment of my professional life. To make that verse immortal in red an' yaller letters among the granite hills was cert'nly a glorious thought. That day I bought a light ladder an' all the needful fixin's, an' made every preparation for my masterpiece of work.

"There was a young chap that came that night to the hotel. He called himself Smith; an' he was such a pleasant sort of fellow that I went, like a blamed fool, an' told him my whole plan, showed him my jinted ladder, an' let him know that the next afternoon I was to do the work. 'Capital,' says he; 'I'm in the business myself,' says he, 'an' I'd like to go up with you, only I've another engagement.' Well, the next mornin', when I got up, there were my ladder, my paints, an' my brushes all gone clean. I hunted everywhere, an' finally ran down the road, looked up to the ledge, an' there was Smith on the little shelf, just finishin' a hideous great big ST. It was enough to make a man faint,— in the first place, to think of the trick; an' in the second, to think of disfigurin' the landscape with sech a vile daub. I bolted my breakfast, took my six-shooter, an' started up the long, steep climb. When I got to the top, I crawled carefully down to the edge an' looked over; there was the ladder at one end an' that scamp was at the other. Quick as a cat, I pulled the ladder up, an' then leanin' over, said, 'My pious young friend, how long do you s'pose you can live on a pint of ile an' a quart or so of paint?' He started back, an' nearly fell off. 'What,' says he, 'you don't mean to leave me here, do you?' 'P'r'aps not,' says I, 'I'm thinkin' of pitchin' you off at once.' 'Well,' says he sulkily, 'you've rather got the best of me. What will you take to let me up?'

"Now, I'd seen that he was a pretty fair workman, so I said, 'You paint out your ST. JOSEPHUS'S LINIMENT, an' put on this poem in real good style.' I showed him the right colors, an' he went at it, swearin' like a pirate, but workin' well, while I sat above, smokin', an' enjoyin' a capital lunch he had brought up.

"Along towards night, he sung out, ' It's all done; jest hand down the ladder.' 'Keep cool, my young friend,' says I, with becomin' gravity, 'don't be violent, an' lemme look at your work.' I had to look at it head downwards, an' couldn't see the last line at that; but the letters seemed bright an' clear, so I let him come up, speakin' significantly of the six-shooter all the while. It was almost dark when we got down to the foot of the hill, an' strain my eyes all I could, the inscription couldn't be read.

" ' Now, Smith,' says I, as we walked up to the hotel, 'I don't bear you any malice, an' we'll eat a good hearty supper together.' 'No,' says he; 'I've got to take the night train down, an' it'll be here in ten minutes.' 'Well,' says I, 'good-by, my boy, and remember not to brag much over your day's picnic.'

" The next mornin' I walked down the road to see my work. You may know how a man swells when he sees his first poem in print; and here was my poem in letters three foot high, on a page of solid rock. My bosom inflated some,—well, I guess; an' hopes of a big rise in my salary began to boom. Just at the turn of the road where the ledge could be seen stood a number of village people, an' they were a-larfin' and a-pintin' at the hill as though it was somethin' ridic'lous. I looked proudly up an' began to read:

> " ' O stranger, when your locks get fewer,
>   And when thereby you've been appalled,
>   Buy the Egyptian Hair Renewer,
>   And by its use grow wholly bald ! ! ! !'

"Well, here's a smooth chance for me; glad to have met you, sir. Won't you stop an' see a little dec'ratin'? No? Well, good day."

C. R. Clapp, '84.

AN INDIAN LEGEND.

I AM a member of '85, and am, moreover, of a romantic and poetical disposition. By chance I was present at that memorable Athletic Meeting, where the noble savages appeared in all their glory, the fire of inborn intelligence gleaming in their eyes, and music of native eloquence flowing from their lips. I always had a passion for Indians; that sight increased it to a perfect frenzy. I resolved to become personally acquainted with an Indian, or die. But how? Alas, I knew not!

During the April recess I went home. I reside in a lovely little village in the far West. As I entered the town, I saw all the fences and unoccupied houses covered with highly colored representations of animals unknown to natural history, and upon inquiry I discovered that there was to be a circus that night. I was just turning away in disgust when a thought struck me: perhaps they had an Indian. That evening found me seated in the front row of the reserved "orchestra chairs," anxiously watching every new arrival into the ring. At last they came — two Indians! How can I describe that frightful war-dance? I covered my eyes with both hands and shuddered. Finally, the long performance was over, and I, with the courage of desperation, followed one of the red men out into the menagerie tent, whither he withdrew. As soon as we were out of sight of the crowd, I accosted him. "Brother," said I, "thy white kinsman brings thee the offering of the peace-pipe of friendship. My name is Solde; what is thine?"

"Me muchee big Injun," said the savage gravely; "no talk much English. Me name is Pottawama Karagdigs, which manes Moighty Chief-Who-Sits-Heavily-In-A-Chair-All-Day."

I plied him with other questions, to which he replied very briefly, in extreme broken English; indeed, he appeared altogether unwilling to enter into conversation with me. But I still had a resource left. I had expected this taciturnity, the distinguishing trait of all Indians, and, knowing the great national weakness, had provided myself with an appropriate remedy.

"Come, brother," I said, "let us recline upon this pile of empty boxes, and converse with open hearts together. I have here that which will quench our thirst when our lips become parched from talking."

Here I drew a bottle from my pocket.

"Ach, whuskey, is it?" cried the savage, delighted. "I mane fire-wather, av coorse. You belly good white man. Me like you much. Lo, the poor Injun will drink."

And he did. When he detached the bottle from his lips, his face was radiant with smiles. I felt much flattered by my success. Here I was vis-a-vis with a friendly disposed Indian. O rapture!

"Does the noble red man feel sad and lonely far from the wigwams and bones of his ancestors?" I inquired.

The savage looked deeply perplexed, but said nothing.

"Would it please my dear brother to tell me a legend of his tribe?"

The savage scratched his head, and then resorted to the bottle. Apparently he drew an inspiration from it, for he brightened up immediately and replied :

"A lagind, is it? Will, I guiss I can. A lagind of the ould country?"

"Yes, an Indian legend."

"Ach, yis; I furgot. The rid, bloody Injun will tell his paceful brithren, which gave him fire-wather, a lagind of his home. Wanst upon a toime, in ages which has long since gone by, there lived among the Corkotahs, which is my tribe, a very powerful chief whose bravery in war was aquilled ounly by his great personal attractions. His name was Dinnis O'Hoy, which manes Ruler-of-the-Fiery Wathers. An' in truth it was a proper name; for niver before among the virtuous Corkotahs was there a man so fond o' takin' a drap o' the crathur (which is an Injun name for fire-wather, ye know)."

Here Pottawama stopped to take a drop himself, and then continued with new vigor :

"Will, an' it came to pass among the paceful Corkotahs, that this chief's visits to the Midicine Man was so fraquint (the Prohibition Law bein' in force in this tribe, there wasn't any tavern-wigwam, so he had to go to the Midicine Man) — his visits was so fraquint, that by and by his property was all gone, and the divil — I mane the Manito — a bit was lift but his ould fiddle. Will, wan day he was wanderin' sadly up an' down the river bank, playin' on his fiddle an' feelin' so thirsty that he was on-certain whither to drink up the river or drown him-silf in it, whin the Avil Shpirit o' Darkniss, attracted by the music, bobbed up seranely from the lower ragions."

"'Will, Dinnis,' ses he, 'ould boy,' ses he, 'ye look down in the mouth,' ses he.

"'Yis,' ses Dinnis, 'it's a sorra day whin I took to drinkin'. Me money's all gone, an' I'd betther be drownin' mesilf as soon as possible,' ses he.

"'Come, Dinnis, be a man,' ses the shly ould div — Shpirit o' Avil. 'I'll till ye what to do. I'll give ye all the money an' all the drink ye want for wan year, if ye'll promise to come wid me at the ind o' that toime.'

"'It'll be a could day for me,' ses Dinnis, 'whin I make such a bargain as that,' ses he.

"'Sure an' ye're quite mishtaken,' ses the divil, 'it'll be entirely the opposite o' that same. We don't have could days down there,' ses he. An' he grinned till the river ran backward wid fright at his ugliness.

"Will, what could poor Dinnis do? He had no money an' no drink, an' so he had to give in; an', faith, I don't blame him much, ather. Will, all that year Dinnis was happy. Ye see, he had all the money he wanted, an' he was drunk from wan ind o' the year to the other. But whin the last day was drawin' near, he grew worried loike, an' sobered down a little, till at last he was so scared that he wint to a howly father, an' tould him the houl story.

"'Will, Dinnis,' ses the howly man, 'ye don't deserve to be saved; but shtill I won't judge ye too harshly,' ses he, 'because I moight ha' done the same under loike timptation,' ses he, shmackin' his lips.

"Thin he wint to a cupboard an' took out a large bottle, which he gave to Dinnis.

"'Take this, Dinnis,' ses he. 'It's the Liquor o' Purification. Just take a drink o' that Liquor an' nivermore can ye go or be took by ony manes to — to — will, to the ragions that's furthest removed from the Happy Huntin' Grounds,' ses he. 'But,' ses he solemnly, 'if ye iver lit another drap o' the crathur pass yer lips, the power o' the Liquor o' Purification will be completely destroyed an' can niver be reshtored. Onybody but yersilf, Dinnis O'Hoy,' ses he, 'moight take all he wanted widout hurtin' the charrum at all, at all; but ye've been such a sinner that way, Dinnis, that ye'd shpile iverything by takin' the laste bit.'

"Dinnis promised niver to touch ony more whuskey, an' afther takin' a shwig o' the Purification, which was moighty bitther shtuff, he wint off perfectly happy, wid the bottle in his pocket.

"He hadn't gone far whin whom should he mate but the ould divil himself.

"'The top o' the mornin' to ye, Dinnis,' ses he; 'are ye drissed in yer Sunday clothes, riddy to make me a little visit?' ses he, wid an ugly shmile.

"'Will, Misther Divil,' ses Dinnis, 'thankin' ye koindly fer yer thoughtful invitation, I'm suff'rin' a little just now from an overdose o' the Liquor o' Purification, an' I guiss I won't throuble ye at prisint,' ses he.

"Whin the divil heard that, he roared an' tore loike a mad bull, an' shwore till the grass was scorched an' the sky turned grane. But he couldn't do nothin'.

"'I'll be avin wid ye yit, Dinnis, ye mane ould chate,' ses he, an' disappeared.

"Dinnis, he laughed till he almost shplit, an' thin wint home. Will, for some time he lived as gay as a lark, but purty soon his ould love for drink began to tormint him. At first he satisfied himself wid carryin' a little bottle o' the crathur in his pocket, an' lookin' at it whin he was dry; but at last he couldn't shtand it ony longer, an' took a little shwig. In a wink the divil was there.

"'Ye've done it now, Dinnis,' ses he, 'an' ye can't get away from me this toime; be quick,' ses he.

"'Will,'' ses Dinnis, good-natured loike, 'ye've caught me fair this toime, haven't ye? But lit's be good frinds shtill,' says he. 'Come, take a drap before we shtart out.'

"'I will, Dinnis, an' I'm glad to see ye behave so sinsibly.'

"But Dennis, the rogue, inshtid o' handin' him the crathur, shlipped into his hand the Liquor o' Purification, an' the divil, suspictin' nothin', took a great shwig.

"'Och, murther,' ses he, 'that isn't whuskey!'

"'No,' ses Dennis shmilin' shwately, 'that's the Liquor o' Purification. An' now, ye ould hathen, ye can't get back to the lower ragions yersilf, an' under the circumstances,' ses he, 'I'm willin' to go wid ye wheriver ye can take me.'

"'Howly cat!' ses the divil.

"He shtood a little while shtunned loike at findin' himsilf suddintly homeliss an' orphaned, as it were, but purty soon he said:

"'Will, Dinnis, me boy, betwane you an' me the infarnal ragions isn't the plisantest place in the wurruld to live in; an' though ye've robbed me o' my home,' ses he, wipin' away a tear, 'I'll forgive ye an' niver throuble ye ony more.'

"Thin he gave Dinnis slathers o' money, an' flew away. Dinnis put it in his pockets, wint home, an' lived iver aftherwards loike a king. An' as for the poor ould divil, not bein' able to foind his way home again, he has to wander about the wurruld an' arn his livin' by sillin' the Liquor o' Purification as patent midicine."

C. H. Grandgent, '83.

"ISE GWINE TER PUFF DEM WEED."

THE name of Jefferson Cæsar Junison is not so well known in history as might be imagined from its dignified two-thirds. He is contemporaneous with his historian, and lives in a very unpretentious house in the city suburbs.

If he were in the gay social circles, the devotees of which his respected father, Mr. Washington Clay Junison, drives about in blazing livery, seated upon his four-wheeled throne, he would probably have his cards engraved "J. Cæsar Junison," as his mother, who presides over a few select tubs for the highly respectable families in the West End, has called him "Ceesawh" from dimpled babyhood to the present curly-headed boyhood.

The pronunciation of this appellation varies with the circumstances under which she addressed him.

Had he been particularly well-behaved and obedient, she murmured a soft "Cee—ee—sa—awh" in a long diapason, patting his woolly pate; but if the occasion were the celebration of some misdemeanor, the diapason stop was closed, and a deep baritone growled "Cezah!" and the caress was substituted by a series of rapid and effective cuffs.

The story I have to tell is the history of this illustrious youth on the day when young patriotism finds vent for enthusiasm in the fire-cracker and torpedo.

The facts were these. On the morning of this eventful holiday, Cæsar, having drawn on his mother's generosity to the extent of ten cents, met his very intimate friend Zeke on his outward stroll, and addressed the following conversation to him, jingling meanwhile the precious dime in his pocket: "Hello, Zeke! is you gwine ter raise eny coin terday?"

"Coin!" exclaimed Zeke; "wal, ef I isn't, I'd like ter know what the reason am ob it. Ise done gone flush wid a dime dis minnit!"

Upon which information they immediately set to work devising the most enjoyable way of lavishing their capitals; and the end was accomplished by the following questions and replies:

"Say, Cees, has you got a pipe?"

"What foh?"

"Case Ise gwine ter puff dem weed."

Accordingly they purchased two clay pipes and some Virginia Leaf, and sought the seclusion of a capacious dry-goods box, standing empty on the sidewalk at the outskirts of the city, and here enjoyed an all-day smoke, puffing their present cares away, and not heeding those of an immediate future.

Mrs. Eliza Junison, arrayed in gorgeous blues and greens, with a black-feathered, yellow-ribboned hat, stood on the threshold of Junison Mansion ready to welcome her only child. Her smile was generous: so was Cæsar's. She greeted him lovingly:

"Cee—ee—sa—awh, you an' me an' you' fader we's gwine on a brief excursion down de riber dis ebenin'. Reckon you kin take dem pennies I gib you dis mo'nin' and git a qua't ob peanuts down on the co'ner befo' we sta't."

This proposition was productive of joy at first, but the sudden way in which she offered Cæsar an opportunity to invest his "coin" filled his heart with terror, as the pennies had been puffed away during the day. So he began stammering an unintelligible answer. The soothing diapason was gradually growing into the deeper baritone in a series of vowel sounds.

"Ceezah, hab you been a-smokin' dis yah day?" asked she with great solemnity.

"I waz wid Zeke," said Cæsar, humbly, "an' he war a-smokin', an' I puffed dem weed jes a small heap, an'"—

"Dar," broke in Mrs. Junison, "dar, dat am enuf"; and, looking alternately at Cæsar and the sky, which was growing sympathetic in shade and tone, she added, "it's mighty wal dar am a sto'm brewin', else you'd go down the riber noway nohow,"—which moved Cæsar to congratulate himself on a supposed escape from coming in contact with his "fader's walken-stick," and to compliment the weather.

There ensued a long soliloquy on the part of Mrs. Junison, wherein she bewailed the waywardness of her only child. Cæsar may have been touched by the affectionate epithets applied to himself, but he showed in no way his sorrow, and only clutched his fingers closer about the clay pipe in his trousers' pocket. Whereupon Mrs. Junison closed our story in the following allegory:

"Ceesah, youse a ben doin' w'at you had no bizness at. Youse ben a-smokin'. Youse a done gone spent dat money foh tobacy. Youse ben a bad

rascal. You take down you' fader walken-stick. I
needs sunfin to 'stain myself wid. Ise gwine to
accoun' to you de mystologographical biography ob
Jubitah's boy, who done gone smokin' w'en he had
no right."

The storm outside was creating a great noise
with the shutters of Junison Mansion, the spatter-
ing of the rain and the thunder vying with Mrs.
Junison's now high-sounding baritone. She seemed
to catch an inspiration from it, and proceeded:

"Dah's no joke abowet dis heah; 'tis an eb'ry-
day fac'. De vary sucumstance w'at Ise a gwine
foh to tell you am a-happenin' dis heah vary sukend.

"Dah war a man name Jupitah, w'at had a boy
name Sto'm, who use foh to skip out an' run away
foh to smoke. He war a tarer. Dar war no man
cud cotch him noway nohow. He war bad. One
fine day he fader miss him, an' putten on he specs
he saw him down de road a-lighten his pipe wid de
'Lightnin' Match,'— de same as we's a-usin' terday,— an' ses Jub to hissef, ses he, 'Ise gwine to
whoop dat coon when he come in'; but he diden
wait. He jes take up his walken-stick, like dis yar
one, an' run aftah dat a boy till he neah los' his
win', an' he cotch him by de collah an' bresh him
bah back till he howl an' a-howl an' a-howl jes like
he's ben a-doin' now, an' de teahs war a-fallin' jes
like dey is at dis minnit. Ceesah, take off dat a
wasecote. Ise gwine ter expashiat on dis subjec' in
a practical mannah, aftah de approve custom ob de
anshents."

Carrying out her threat, the loud cracks of the
walking-stick, the yells of Cæsar, and the advisory

remarks of Mrs. Junison played a loud finale to the tune that had started with the song,

"Ise gwine ter puff dem weed."

F. D. Sherman, '87·

" In olde days of the king Artour
All was this loud fulfilled of faerie.
The Elf quene with hire joly compagnie
Danced full oft in many a grene mede.
The grete charite and prayeres
Of limitoures and other holy freres
This maketh that ther ben no faerie."

SOME owe it to Carlyle and Emerson and the
bloodless transcendentalists, and some thank
Professor Bowen and the easily contented Scotch
metaphysicians, for the fact that such a Paradise as
the Mussulman looks forward to is no longer for us.
The fancy and the affections find nothing better to
linger around with us in the ruggedness of American
business life than college memories. Our visions
are still firelight pictures in Holworthy rooms. We
think less, virtuous and logical as we were taught
to be, of fair-ankled Hebe and of damsels with a
dulcimer. For us it is better to let the mind run
back to the well-bred beauties who came to our Class
Days and wandered on the green. The pulse thrills
still with the memories of triumphs over Yale, on
the Field and on the Lake, when the college
" Hurrah " told of proud victories. It is hard,
therefore, to realize that there was something which
needed righting in the kingdom of Harvard twenty
years ago.

To Harvard men of the years from 1860–1870
college memories are especially rich and varied.
Youths of noble spirit were going to the war and
coming back with tales of glory, or dying, to leave

immortal names to be recorded in Memorial Hall. When Dr. Peabody gave his last warning and blessing " to those about to go forth into the battle of life," his words had a very present meaning. Rustication was no more a terror but a ready release from the objection of parents to joining the army. When Hazard Stevens was suspended for screwing in his tutor in Greek, did he not thereby shortly become the youngest general in the Grand Army? Did it profit that fellows should spend the fleeting years in delving out the stories of ancient worthies, fellows who knew Robert Shaw, and the Lowells, and Barlow, and the two Hallowells, and hundreds like them? Cambridge girls did not recommend the ancients as sole exemplars of the fashion of men who could win them. But they told of the reply which his true-love gave to General Bartlett when he wrote to her: "My dear, it breaks my heart: but there is so little left of me that I think I ought to offer to release you from your engagement." Her answer was: "So long as there is enough left to bear the name of Frank Bartlett, he is the only man I want to marry."

The war spirit was in the college both before and after the war. One famous colonel of cavalry had three claims on fame in the Freshman myths. He had been stroke of the crew, he had cut a very huge rebel from shoulder to hip, and previously he had fearlessly sent our chapel Bible to Yale and likewise endowed our chapel with Yale's Bible. And after the war E. W. F. complained in the ADVOCATE that the Faculty had not the sense to realize that "the same blood was spent" in some midnight college exploit "which watered the plains of Gettysburg and in front of Battery Wagner." Seriously, there was where the first trouble began. The Faculty had little knowledge of, or sympathy with, the students. They were far more ancient men than the active professors of today. Harvard especially invited to Commencement "the venerable ministers who have a parish." Of that class of guests many abided. They were good men, something more or less than human. Some Yale men are saying now that they have too many such, and too few others. By the way, one of your old editorials about some Yalensian discussions is righteously entitled "Small fowles maken melodie." The contemporaries of the early editors of the *Collegian* and the ADVOCATE were ripened for the war-time, and when they were partially ripe there was no war. They had to attack some wrongs. Nobody of account did otherwise then. They pitched into the ancient errors nearest at hand. Out of this came the ADVOCATE, the story of whose beginning the present editors ask for. There were errors. It was wrong to force men daily before light in winter and thrice on Sundays to religious services. It seemed a bitter error that irreligion and profanity should thus be fostered. The President himself was a grievous error. The change, first to Dr. Peabody and later to President Eliot, of itself was enough to mark the dawning of a new and better day. The educational and religious system was hostile to its subjects as a thing of another day always is.

Those were the days to burst the bonds. The

college was ready to become a great university. Some of the men and all of the rules were cramping the destiny of Harvard. They were not of the size of the times. How could the flock look upon the shepherds as intellectual leaders when the office of the professors most closely brought home to the students was to take marks from the scholarship of such as kept a dog, or wore other than a black coat on certain days, or rejected oatmeal metaphysics, or walked on the grass, or pared the nails, or went to sleep in the cold chapel? The professors thus did their duty as ordained of old in the college laws.

Students were treated, or operated on, upon ancient general principles, without any recent reflections as to methods. *Experimentum in corpore vili* had always been a scholastic precept. The student in America had never been asked how he thought it worked on him and never took occasion to tell until the *Collegian* and ADVOCATE were founded. This was the object of their beginners. Perhaps the fight was precipitated on the part of the Lilliputs by the act of the one of the professors who was suspected of being against the war and in favor of slavery. In a moment of irritation he called some of the blood of " Battery Wagner " by a name such as boys apply to one another. Their class, '67, was a class of marked individuality and independence. Soon after the three numbers of the *Collegian* were printed. These contained nothing more revolutionary than a remark ascribed to Socrates : " How many were worshipping in the agora ? " Glaucon : " One, indeed." Socrates :

"Forsooth, tomorrow I will sooner attend a roll call." This was written by the poet editor. Sanborn, the second editor, then first scholar in his class, and one of the most conservative of men, wrote: "It seems a profanity to make the worship of God a mere instrument of police service." The other editor, the present writer, wrote: "We want some place and opportunity for the students to meet and become acquainted with the professors. The college has suffered in no small degree for the want of this." Later the other weighty matters above mentioned were likewise discussed. But the beginning sufficed. The three editors were ordered to discontinue the *Collegian.* The college was roused instantly. Everybody wanted to be an editor. The captain of the crew and the captain of the nine tendered physical backing. Possibly the presidents of some of the religious societies offered solace or support. There was no hesitation. E. W. F., the best all-around man of our time, and F. P. S., son worthy of the father who equipped John Brown, and M. W. (all ready to become a later leader of the Mugwumps), joined two of the *Collegian's* editors in founding the ADVOCATE. The motto of the first was *"Dulce est periculum"*; of the second, *"Veritas nihil veretur."* When the Faculty formally decided on expulsion, and announced it, it gave a moment's regret for the old folks at home, but roused a little Spartan feeling likewise, something in replica of the war spirit, something large for the occasion. The ludicrous features are now the plainest. Youth will out. The writer was sixteen. The older and wiser editors were three years older. Some of the new editors' friends pasted the posters announcing the birth of the ADVOCATE on the President's house, and on University Hall steps, and on the Elms. Lucky it was for the editors that as at Troy the powers above took sides. On the side of the juveniles, Dr. Holmes, Dr. Hedge, Colonel Higginson, F. B. Sanborn, Professors Gurney, Child, Cutler, and all the younger alumni, declared themselves. James Russell Lowell, they heard, attended a Faculty meeting in the martyrs' behoof. He certainly said to them: "I was something of a revolutionist myself, you know." They doubted if Leonidas had ever received so congenial a tribute. Professor Child gave out "Free Speech" as the subject for the next forensic, told us to say our say on it, and in a humorous and lovable way added, that for his part he thought that boys must have some safety-valve or they might explode. For two years the students printed their thoughts about themselves and their government before the first editors graduated, and for eighteen years since. One of the many like articles of those early days is headed: "MURDERER: We are men, my liege! MACBETH: Aye, in the catalogue ye go for men." Dr. Hedge and others wrote notable essays on our themes, and the Doctor the same year had the Phi Beta Kappa oration, and in stronger words than ours said: "The professors are police officers. Harvard must be made a university." And Harvard, under President Eliot's glorious administration, did shortly become a great university. The ADVOCATE was the first of college newspapers. Many others followed. Can they not profitably advocate now the cheapening of education and living at Harvard? Is it not the one blot on President Eliot's administration that in effect the result will be an attempt to gather grapes from bramble bushes only, that is, an attempt to make scholars only out of such as could live in Beck and Weld, and to bar the sons of impecunious literary and professional men whose blood is quite as hopeful of results in scholarship? Neither is it American to say our boys can be sizars or servitors.

College magazine poetry used to be from all too hollow reeds, always excepting Dr. Holmes'. Some critic with a heart should tell you how the Advocate Poets, in the ADVOCATE and in the *Century*, *Harper's*, and *Life*, and elsewhere, rhyming of love, as it is or used to be, and writing of life without pathos, have founded the first purely native and natural school of American poets. This is not too much to say of the verses of Frederic Loring, Soley, Fiske, Pease, Goodwin, Robert Grant, Scollard, Sherman, Lord, Kittredge, Gates, Nutter, and the forty others, who, since the time of Gage, E. J. Lowell, E. C. Clarke, F. P. Stearns and Leonard of '67, have made your verses.

W. G. Peckham, '67.

THEN AND NOW.

EXTRACT FROM THE JOURNAL OF A PARS FUI.

FIRST night at Harvard, after a most exciting day. Took a car to Oak Square instead of Harvard Square; tardy to the first recitation; wrote home for an excuse; bought a lounge for a dollar and a quarter; saw a man that I think must be the President; subscribed to the *Lampoon, Crimson, Register, Echo, Herald* and ADVOCATE; ordered a tall hat; drew a fine room in Divinity Hall; did not have time to call on the members of the corporation; decided to work at least nine hours a day; am going in for honors.

First examination today. Proctor wore squeaky boots, read newspapers, looked over my shoulder, and couldn't explain the paper. Know I made a rush; had a lot of things learned by heart. One question was: "What county of England is nearest to France?" My answer was:

> "The farther 'tis from England,
> The nearer 'tis to France,
> Then turn not pale, beloved snail,
> But come and join the dance."

Am going in for honorable mention.

Have joined the Harvard Foot-ball Club, Harvard University Boat Club, Harvard Base-Ball Club, and Harvard Athletic Association. Hope to get on the crew and the nine. May perhaps go to

THEN AND NOW.

EXTRACT FROM THE JOURNAL OF A PARS FUI.

ANOTHER year begun. Usual number of inquiring Freshmen and admiring sisters. Was there ever a time when I had to ask the way to the Bursar's office? Representatives of the college papers in search of new victims blundered into my room. Time taken up with students' calls. Arranged a schedule of work for the year. Shall not try to do more than six hours a day of hard study;—am resolved to be moderate.

Semi-Annual examination, always a bore. The proctor said he had answered ninety-six questions, sharpened fourteen pencils, and lent two stylographs—he finally went to sleep. Began to read the examination books tonight. Usual number of literal quotations from my lectures, and a few poor jokes. Examinations are at best a necessary evil, but they should be less so, if men would take more pains to arrange their thoughts systematically. Am resolved to read all the books within a month.

Have been requested to subscribe for the "eight," the "nine," the "eleven," the "twelve," and other arithmetical organizations. Have one stereotyped answer: "I believe in college sports and believe in supporting them; I will with pleasure give what I the gymnasium, but it is such a stuffy little place, and then it is not good form to go regularly. Am going in for athletics.

ADVOCATE out today, with my letter on " Where are the plank walks?" I wonder why the Faculty pay so little attention to student opinion. My letter looks well in print. Am going in for college journalism.

First meeting of the new ADVOCATE board. To me were assigned two columns of items. This paper work will help me very much in themes and in English courses. Am going in for a lively narrative style.

Thank goodness, the last number of the ADVO-CATE is off our hands; spent three days this week on it. Of course we have had a good deal of influence on college opinion here, and have set a standard of creditable college journalism for other parts of the country. But we have had to sacrifice time, strength, and college rank. I am going in for a degree if I can get it.

can afford, provided you will render to me, and the other subscribers, a complete, itemized, business account of all your expenditures."

Got my feet wet today crossing the yard on the way to Faculty meeting. Why does not the corporation grant us plank walks? The students seem to hold us responsible. Have half a mind to write to the *Advertiser* about it.

First proofs of the article on "Causes and Prevention of Infant Pauperism"; also a hint from the editor that it "seems to lack dignity." I suppose that comes of neglecting the work in English when I was in college.

Am asked to write for the ADVOCATE once more. With all my heart! The work for that paper was one of the most valuable things in my college course. To be sure, it had much less effect on the college world than we supposed; but the association, the practical work, the experience of managing men and things, was worth more than any two courses, and was one of the elements which made a degree represent real mental growth.

Albert Bushnell Hart, '80.

PHRYNE: A PHANTASY.

SOFTLY, softly, my lady — quiet now — here we are. This is our car — the gilded one with the plush carpetings. See! This is your ladyship's cushion, and your ladyship's rug; and there is another cushion for Achmet; all that can make us comfortable for an afternoon's journey. In with you! Don't stand blinking at the sun in that lazy way! . . . Why do they make these doors so hard to open? . . . They are waiting for us. . . . Now you're in. . . . Wait till I get this clumsy door fastened. . . . All right here! . . . We're off, my lady; and you are lying there on your rug as if you were unconscious that you were the pet leopardess of his gracious majesty the Sultan, and that I was your ladyship's slave.

You're like all the rest of the sex, my lady, you're captivating, and you're deceitful. To look at you now, who would even suspect that you could tear and kill — me, perhaps,— if the whim seized you? Who would guess how you shriek and scream if one of your slaves forgets to bring you your mid-day meal at its usual time? Nobody, Phryne. There's no denying, either, that you're a handsome creature; and no one is more aware than you of your personal advantages. Look, madam, you are as glossy as a mirror, and your spots glow like coals of fire; your claws are as white as the petals of the Neringhi-flower; your teeth are like pearls; your little tongue is red as the coral; and you are so used to being told this, and to being smoothed and caressed,

that you would die of jealousy did I forget to pet
you; and you pretend to be very indifferent to
flattery.

We've been a long time together, my lady. Do
you remember when we first met? No; you were
too young for that. A poor hunter of the Kowambé,
I used to wander for days among the craggy hills
of Algiers, in search of game. On one of these
journeys I came unexpectedly upon a little family
group: you and a brother kitten were playing about
your mother, who regarded you with grave pride.
My match-lock was never aimed so truly, never
poised so firmly. Your mother fell at the discharge, stark dead; and in abject terror you and
your brother clung to her lifeless body, spitting and
glaring at me as I came clambering over the rocks.
I grasped you without fear, however, and tossed
you hastily into a fold of my dress, while I stripped
off your mother's beautiful skin. Then I hurried
on, up rough hills, through deep forests, over burning sands, till I came to the village of our tribe;
for I dreaded the wrath of your father. You, poor
girl, nearly perished by the way, for you were too
young to taste aught but milk, and there was naught
in my wallet but a scrap of dried goat's flesh and a
handful of dates. At the end of the second day of
our journey we reached the village; your brother
was dead, and you were almost a skeleton,— and
so weak!

How fast we are going! Does it disturb you,
my lady? See how we are rocking from side to
side, and see the trees and the bushes, how they
fly past! You were frightened the first time we

rode together in one of these trains. You lay
crouched in the corner and waved your tail slowly
from side to side, as you do when you are angry;
your eyes gleamed wildly, and you gave little low
growls of anger and terror. Achmet was frightened,
too; he had never been in a train; his head swam
and he grew dizzy; he threw himself down in a
corner and prayed to Allah; and then he crouched
up close to you, Phryne, my lady, and he buried
his face in your soft fur and moaned; and you
comforted him, and he comforted you, till the
journey was over.

Where was I in your history? Oh, yes; I
brought you to the village, no longer savage, but
O so weak and thin! However, plenty of warm
goat's milk quieted your cries, and under the influence of rest and petting you grew sleek and playful,
and became the admiration of the tribe. Beautiful
and entertaining as you were, you did not occupy
all Achmet's thoughts; for Achmet was in love.
The fairest girl of the Kowambé filled his soul with
fire and his eyes with longing; and she returned
his love. She admired him for his nimbleness and
his courage, and his skill in the chase, which made
him distinguished among the youths of the tribe;
and the sight of her bright smile and her lustrous
eyes caused Achmet's heart to beat wildly and his
cheeks to flame as she passed by him on the way to
the well with the other maidens. She saw you, my
lady, and admired you. What would I not have
given to her,—my beloved one? You had been
my constant companion for a year, and we loved
each other dearly; but I loved her even better,

and I led you to her tent one evening and returned without you.

Fetnah's father frowned on my suit. He was a crabbed dotard, no richer and no better than the rest of our tribe; but the son of the sheik was my rival, and the old man favored him; and on my account you received spurnings and abuse which even the caresses of the kindest of mistresses could not atone for. Now, when you were nearly two years old and quite grown, I despaired more and more from day to day of softening the heart of the father. As a desperate resort I left the tribe and went to Tangier, determining to become rich or never to return. I toiled from day to day in the bazaars; I sold all my stock of skins — including your mother's; I bore ill usage without a murmur; neglecting myself that I might bring back more to the insatiable old man.

Fortune favored me. At the end of a year, I was richer than I had dared to hope,— richer than any man in the village,— and with joy in my heart I hurried back, and an hour before the daybreak of my second day's journey I saw the huts of our people nestling under the shadowy palm trees in the gray morning. You, Phryne, were the first familiar sight which met my eyes; but not as you were,— no! A rough cord tethered you to a palm tree. Beside you was a rude kennel, and bones and scraps lay scattered on the ground around it. You slept; but ever and anon you growled and stirred uneasily in your sleep as if savage thoughts were troubling your mind. I spoke to you. You leaped and fawned upon me in an ecstasy of delight, and

tried to devour me with caresses. Overjoyed as I
was to see you once more, I was lost in indignation
at the wretch who had dared to maltreat my Phryne.
My dirk flashed from my belt in a moment, and cut
the rough rope which chafed my girl's neck — and
she was free. Hardly had I done this when a
mocking voice said close to my ear: " You have returned, then? Well, you may have your beggarly
cat, but take her away with yourself; the sheik's
'wife has no charity for such outcasts!" I was
stunned for a moment . . . and then . . . rage
and jealousy made a demon of me . . . my knife
was yet in my hand . . . it was but the work of a
moment . . . it was buried to the hilt in my rival's
breast!

He fell without a groan, and you sprang on him
and would have drunk his blood; but I dragged
you away. All that night we journeyed, and all
the next day, fleeing from the vengeance which
pursued us. Crouched on the saddle-bag of my
camel, you consoled me in my bitter despair. The
glitter in your eyes as you thought of your late
tormentor changed to a look of savage joy as you
remembered him lying there, stark and stiff, on the
sand; my gaze answered yours; and together we
mourned over the lost mistress and rejoiced over
the fallen foe. We reached Tangier, we embarked
for Constantinople on the first ship which left the
port (for our enemies were hard upon us), and
within a week's time we were wandering, homeless
and friendless, in the streets of the sacred city.
Here one of his gracious majesty's pashas saw you
and admired your beauty. We were summoned

before the vizier. The Sultan demanded your price. I replied that you were his majesty's already, and begged to be allowed to remain your slave and his. He smiled; and you and I became court favorites from that moment.

Yes, Phryne, many are the gracious ladies who have fondled your mottled skin, and your silky ears, and have led you about by your golden collar. The youngest wife of his imperial highness, the peerless Badoura, is inconsolable without you, and —

Il Allah! What has happened? Mohammed save us; we are wrecked! O my beauty, my pet, are you hurt? There is a beam crushing your back to the floor. Let me try to lift it. . . . It is too heavy . . . I will stoop; let me try it so. . . . Gently, gently. . . . O merciful Allah! Let me go! . . . Phryne, let me go, I say! . . . Do you hear me, madam? Let me go! . . . Help! Help! Help! . . . Come, let me go, my lady; it's Achmet, your Achmet. . . . Let me — go. . . . Let me . . . Help! . . . Achmet, my lady . . . your Ach — Oh! —

L. McK. Garrison, '88·

EVENING: A SKETCH.

IT is growing dark in the little Norman fishing village of Grande Roche. The last piece of the great, round sun has just sunk into the water, and now is strangely distinct in the weird half-light, half-gloom which comes between the end of day and the beginning of night. Away to the right, the tall, black cliffs rise up out of the level plain of sand and lose themselves in the darkness beyond. On the left you can follow the wavy line of the beach until it reaches the little port of Dives, whose low, thatched roofs crowd around the little church in a huddled group. In this evening light you can see the golden weather-cock above the inn reflecting back the red of the sky, just as it did when William the Conqueror stopped there before he sailed. Beyond, the fields of yellow colza and wheat, bordered by lines of tall poplars, are turning dark purple.

Back of you, the crooked street of Grande Roche goes along, following the line of the beach. It finally ascends the hill on the left to the old chateau. It stops at the high iron gates, surmounted by bristling griffins, who have been sticking their forked tongues out at each other for centuries past.

Everything is still. The soft summer wind, even, is so gentle that you do not feel it as it passes. The tide comes in late tonight, and the dark sands stretch out before you until they almost reach the soft, tinted clouds the sun has left behind. But just before they reach them, you can see a faint line of white where the breakers are, and a bit of green above.

Pools of water which the sea has left in the hollows of the sands reflect a dead-white light to you, which makes the fishing-boat between, lying on its side, as black as though it had been burned. The moaning of the sea, far out in the distance, comes in to you so softly that it does not break the stillness about you, nor do the sweet tones of the Angelus, which has just ceased ringing.

The curé comes out of the church and locks the door, then walks down the silent street, his wooden-soled shoes making a great clattering on the cobble-stones. But few lights are seen glimmering through the doorways, for all the men-folk of Grande Roche and most of the women are off to the Grand Pêche, drawing in the seine which was planted in the morning. You can see them, mere specks, outlined against the dying day in the west, as they bend to their toil. Père André goes down only to the first house beyond the carved stone fountain which stands in the middle of the street. He stops a moment to inquire if poor old Mère Jacqueline is feeling any easier, and then hastens back to the parsonage, so that he may get his supper in time to meet the good folk as they come back, and give them a word of encouragement.

It is growing dark, and now you can no longer see the glistening weather-cock at Dives. A fresh, cool wind has sprung up from the seaward, and the distant murmur of the waves seems to be growing louder. The sea has turned, and now commences to take possession of the sands again. It reaches in nearer and nearer with every wave it throws for-ward, and with the return of the sea come in the

fishermen and women of Grande Roche. The
baskets, strapped on their brawny shoulders, are
full of fish, and they talk and laugh together as
they come in through the darkness over the cool,
hard sand. Their bare feet splash in the puddles,
and the wind blows forward the short dresses and
loose hair of the women as they walk. As you
stand on the shore, their voices and laughter come
in to you through the night so oddly, in gusts, as
the wind comes and goes, and without echo.

They come up the broad beach and down the
street together, dropping off in pairs and groups as
they reach their homes. Some stop to have a
friendly word with a neighbor as they pass. All
hush their voices as they near poor Mère Jacqueline's door, and speak kind words of the good old
soul who is passing away. For awhile the street is
full of life, and lights stream from every door.
Good Père André is among them, going about with
a pleasant word for all, praising their good fortune,
and asking after each one. Then one by one the
green wooden shutters and quaint oak doors are
closed. *Bon soirs* are said and *bonnes nuits* wished,
and gradually the street becomes quiet again.
Each little house hugs jealously within its embrace
the warmth and happiness of its own hearth. Outside, all is night. The sea has come back, and the
roaring and beating of its waves on the beach gives
again the music without which the village seems
dead.

Morton D. Mitchell, '87.

THE STORY OF A CHARITY SERMON.

THE Reverend Charles Angelo Springer opened the door just enough to put his face outside and to take a little sniff of fresh air as he cast a hurried glance upward at the black and gloomy sky. One glance seemed to satisfy him, for quickly withdrawing his head he hastily readjusted his spectacles, jammed his tall, black hat down more firmly upon his head, drew his cloak closer to his person, and finally, opening the door a little wider, squeezed through the opening, and stood on the steps in the pelting rain. He had no sooner closed the door than he uttered an exclamation of impatience, and rang the door-bell. The old cabman, who was standing with his vehicle before the house, watched the tall, spare figure at the door, and wondered what idea his patron had in remaining there without any sufficient shelter from such severe weather. The reason soon came to light, for, as the servant threw open the door, the reverend gentleman made a sudden dive for a corner near by, and before the maid could recover from her astonishment emerged triumphantly therefrom with an old green cotton umbrella. It was very evident that the Reverend Charles Angelo Springer was absent-minded. This fact seemed to impress both the cabman and the servant-girl, as the expressive grin which appeared on the face of each at the sight of the old umbrella proved beyond question. As Cabby assisted the clerical gentleman to enter the ancient-looking ark, he bestowed a knowing wink upon the maid, who was still lingering in the hallway by the open door.   She, however, tossed her head, apparently in virtuous indignation at such unwarranted familiarity, and closed her door with a bang.   At this, Cabby, who was a sly old boy, and knew the ways of the sex, only grinned quietly and proceeded to mount his box.   But as he gathered up the reins he cast another glance at the house door, behind the panels of which a slight movement of the gauze curtains might be seen, and with a smile winked again, though this time in a more conciliatory fashion.   Then he snapped his whip, and jerked the reins to wake his horse from what, in spite of the rain, appeared to be a sound sleep. Slowly that much-abused animal pulled himself together; slowly the old vehicle rattled down the lonely street; slowly and reluctantly numerous inquisitive neighbors left the windows at which they had placed themselves to witness the departure of the Reverend Charles Angelo Springer from his boarding house.

It was only a few weeks since that young and learned gentleman had been a student at the Divinity School.   He had graduated with high honors, at the head of his class, and had at once received a call to occupy the pulpit of the church in Wehback, his own native place.   It was easy to see that his fellow-townsmen regarded him as a rising man.   There was no doubt that he was a hard student; at the Divinity School, the headquarters of earnest workers, he had been considered a long-haired grind, and it was likewise believed that he was the least practical of them all.   His own reticence seemed to confirm this general belief. While he was not a brilliant scholar, he had great powers of application; this was the explanation of his high standing. But his good qualities were marred, and more than counterbalanced, by an over-weening self-confidence. He was going to convert everybody, the world. People should flock from far and near to hear him preach, and his sermons were to be the wonder of the intelligent and learned.

Shortly after graduation he had been invited to deliver a charity sermon in the city, and had accepted the invitation. When it was explained to him he learned that some charitable society had erected a chapel in one of the worst quarters of the city, and that various young clergymen were in turn invited to expound the word and letter of the Holy Writ to the sinners of that neighborhood. He had accepted with enthusiasm; he wished to make this sermon a kind of test discourse, and had no doubt that he should be entirely satisfied with the result. So he hunted about until he found lodgings in a retired part of the city, where he expected to have quiet, and sat him down to compose his model effort. After working at it for a day or two, at intervals when neither the children were quarrelling nor fighting in the street below, nor the young lady boarder practising " scales " on her piano, nor the Teutonic neighbor vainly trying to make music on his cornet, he finished the masterpiece.

The morning before the day on which he was to preach, the agent of the society had called, and had given him instructions, together with the key of the chapel, and had assured him that a carriage should be sent for him on the morrow. We have seen how the carriage came, and how he entered it and set out for the chapel.

When he alighted before that not very imposing edifice, he suggested to the hack-driver that he should call for him after the service, but as that worthy did not appear to understand him, he repeated the order. To his surprise he discovered that the man was very deaf. However, after some little trouble, he managed to make himself understood, and then, nearly wet through, proceeded to enter the chapel. Within, it was cold and dreary, but he opened wide the door, and then took his place upon the platform to wait for his congregation. As he looked about him he had no doubt that he could easily make himself heard in the farthest corners, and the only thing that troubled him was the thought that he should be obliged to lead the singing.

Meanwhile time passed, and not another person entered the house. The hour for service was half-past ten, but it was already a quarter before eleven, and not a single person had appeared. The Reverend Charles Angelo felt his confidence slowly forsaking him; he should not, after all, have a chance to test his powers.

At eleven o'clock a man entered and took one of the back seats. The Reverend Charles Angelo Springer thanked and blessed that man from the bottom of his pedantic heart, and vowed that even though this one should be his only hearer, he would deliver his sermon. His heart warmed as he thought that he was to be the means of bringing one soul home. In his excitement he replaced upon his nose his wet spectacles, which obscured his vision, and which he had taken off for the express purpose of wiping and cleaning.

He began his sermon. All went well, though he was shocked to observe that his hearer always remained sitting, and never changed his position; even when the prayer was made that person never bowed his head, nor did the hymn which the congregation were to sing cause him to stand. He was pleased to note that at times his audience of one nodded approvingly, and as he neared the end of his remarks, saw with pride that the man was overcome with emotion, and had allowed his head to sink forward upon his breast.

The service over, the Reverend Charles Angelo Springer descended from the platform. Determined to address a few words of encouragement to the new convert, he approached the motionless figure. As he did so, a low, deep, nasal sound met his ear. Was the man really moved as much as that? To move a person to tears was more than he had ever expected, even in his most hopeful moods. Verily, it was a great triumph. He laid his hand gently, possibly a little patronizingly, on the man's shoulder. At his touch the figure gave a start and arose. Where had he seen that face before? There was something strangely familiar in it. All at once the man threw his arms wide apart, and yawned. Then it flashed upon him. No need for him now to listen while the man told him in a loud, high-pitched voice that, as it was so wet outside, he had tied his horse in a shed near by, and had himself come inside, where it was dry, until his patron should be ready to have him drive back to the dingy, musty lodgings. No need for the other to excuse himself for being sleepy. And, above all, there was no need to strike a man when he was down, as Cabby did, when, on drawing up in front of the house in the lonely street, he demanded twice the usual amount of fare — and received it, too. No need, perhaps, to say how great a fall was there, and likewise no need to expatiate longer on the discomfiture of that learned young apostle and revivalist, the Reverend Charles Angelo Springer.

W. Wetherbee, '87.

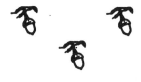

OBSERVATIONS OF A WALLFLOWER.

D EAR Mr. Editor:
The other day, I chanced to take down from
the book-shelves an old copy of the *Lounger*, and
soon became interested in a letter, telling of the state
of society in those days, written by one Marjory
Mushroom, who, as it seems to me, was, after all,
only a very ordinary, commonplace young woman
like myself, and there came into my head the idea
that I, perhaps, might supply the present generation,
if not the future, with a little amusement of a like
character, as I have, for some years, been present
at many parties without taking a very active part in
them, and for this reason I shall call my paper:
Observations of a Wallflower.

Anyone who is sufficiently attracted by my title
to glance over these lines may be interested to know
how I happened to become a wallflower, and why,
realizing that I was one of that unhappy sisterhood,
I still continued to go to parties. The second
question is more easily answered than the first,
though there are doubtless few who will believe me
when I say that I went because I enjoyed myself.
Yet this is nevertheless quite true; only, mind you,
I do not pretend to have enjoyed myself like other
girls. I am not like those young women, who, after
spending the better part of a night with no greater
amount of attention than a couple of hurried turns
with some contrite floor-manager, exclaim in the
dressing-room, after the party is over, "O my dear,

wasn't it too lovely?" "Didn't you have a splendid time?" or "Did you ever know anyone dance so divinely as Mr. T.?"— No, no; I realized quite early that a wallflower must look for her pleasures in something beside dancing and flirting, and as I was clearly fore-ordained by birth and breeding to become a wallflower, so was I mercifully adapted by temperament to enjoy myself in that humble position, and after experiencing my first failure with a sort of stolid disappointment, I immediately set to work to find enjoyment in looking on, and little do the gay butterflies imagine what a very critical old moth it is watching them from her quiet corner.

My first observations were naturally made in the dressing-room, let us say, of Armory Hall, for, since you are a college paper, it may be well to confine myself to that by no means small field of action, the college parties. Some of my sisters may object that it is unfair to tell what I have seen, when their guard was, so to speak, down; and, indeed, if they only knew how few straws it takes to reveal the direction of the wind, I am quite sure they would keep those treacherous little articles more carefully out of sight. For instance, there is that stiff little straw of self-importance. How well I remember the young lady who used to plant herself before the dressing-table, quite as though it stood in her own private apartments, and monopolize the mirror for five or ten minutes at a time, though she made little alteration in her toilet beyond patting down her crimps or picking out her laces. She might have spared herself even that trouble, for she never danced enough in the whole course of an evening to turn a single ruffle.   How different from that rollicking little tomboy, who came night after night, with her clothes only half on, and her hair fastened with two or three pins, which she would draw out and stick in again half-a-dozen times, trying to make them do duty for the dozen that were certainly needed for her curly mop, till someone would suggest that she should help herself from the tray on the dressing-table, which, five minutes later, would be completely empty.   One of the maids was always standing over her till the last moment before she entered the dancing hall, sewing on a slipper bow, catching up a looping, or basting the lace into the bottom of her dress.   She monopolized, too, even more than the superior maiden, but with such sweet, good-natured thoughtlessness, that everyone felt kindly toward her, and when at the last moment she went flying out of the room, with two left-hand gloves, and her sash fringe full of the hayseed of last summer's lawn parties, everyone smiled and hoped she'd have a good time.   There were two girls, both of them belles, who always wore the most superb flowers, and simply in the arranging and handling of these their characters were revealed to me.   One of them, the taller and sweller of the two, would come into the dressing-room, which most of us entered with about as much shape as a feather-bed, with her superb plush wrap reaching nearly to her feet, and her beautiful dress trailing over the uncarpeted entries, a sort of grand advertisement of the fact that she could have another elegant costume tomorrow, if she chose.   Her first act, after bowing to her acquaintances, was to cast her

eye over the row of florists' boxes on one of the
benches; and very seldom was she disappointed in
finding her name on one of the covers. She did
this in such a very matter-of-course way that there
were certain girls who suggested she must have
ordered the flowers herself, but I felt sure this was
a libel.

The other belle was not so generously endowed
with this world's goods. She usually arrived en-
veloped in a big plaid shawl or waterproof, rubber-
boots on her feet and a blue worsted "cloud"
encircling her pretty face. The moment she
entered the room she was besieged by a clamoring
crowd. "Will you lunch with me tomorrow?"
"Can you go to the Symphony concert with me
next Friday?" "Can you help me select a bonnet
tomorrow afternoon?" "Oh! won't you help me
with these flowers?" The last from at least five
girls at once. She had great taste in arranging
flowers, and such perfect good-will in offering or
granting assistance, that nearly all her acquaintances
depended upon her, except the rival belle, whom I
have seen fussing and fuming, pricking her fingers,
tearing her laces, and even stamping her foot in
vexation when the heavy-headed roses or brittle-
stemmed carnations snapped under her rough
handling and came tumbling down onto the dressing-table. The almost lightning rapidity with which
the other girl caught up her flowers and pinned
them onto the front of her dress, always in just the
right place, was something little short of a miracle
to the uninitiated. I suppose she had learned the
knack through long practice and through being

obliged to hurry over her own toilet after spending all the time there was on other people.

Besides these more prominent figures there were others of minor importance, like the girl in her fifth season, who had something ill-natured or ridiculous to say about everybody in the room, and that little bud, equally weak-minded, though less disagreeable, who went about complimenting indiscriminately and admiring every girl in turn. There was the sentimental girl, who was always having "experiences" and times that were "so frightfully awkward, my dear," and who was ready to make a confidant of anyone who would listen to her. Then I mustn't forget the slangy damsel, who spoke of all the "fellows" by their first, and all the matrons by their last names, without the bother of a handle. It was she who always had the latest bit of fashionable scandal, which she retailed in an alarmingly loud tone while pulling off her leggins, and I regret to say that, although she was not a favorite, and the girls were rather afraid of her, her corner of the dressing-room was always surrounded by a crowd of girls, listening, chatting and working on their gloves. But, lest I am accused of lingering too long in the dressing-room, let me hurry out and find someone to take me into the hall.

II.

The music is charming, Cheney's orchestra at its best. It is a waltz they are playing, and one's first thought is how well everyone is dancing. But what is this that comes flying along, dividing the couples and scattering them right and left? Zig-zag he goes, zig-zag, like a bee trying to make his escape. No, he is not mad, the girl who is dancing with him is not alarmed — only a little anxious lest she may not be able to keep up with him. "This is the diagonal," explains my next neighbor to the man at her side. "Does he have it often?" asks the young man.

I could answer him easily that he does, far, far too often; in fact, he has nothing else. The diagonal is very pretty when well executed, and at times it is a convenient method of passing between the whirling couples, but a dancer who can waltz in no other way is certainly very tiresome. Now the red-headed Sophomore comes bounding along, hitching, jerking, stopping short every now and then, but always so penitent and so anxious to try again that his partners only laugh resignedly and submit. He knows his shortcomings, but how can he improve if no one will practice with him? This is so true that all are ready to take their turn with this humble worshipper of Terpsichore. The bandy-legged man already referred to is not so humble, though his dancing(?) is far more trying. Here he comes with that tall girl in pink. Being short himself, he always selects the tallest girls in the room, presumably to make the balance true. At present, the balance is anything but true; he bobs up as the girl comes down, staggers backwards, dragging the unfortunate girl after him; she sees an approaching couple and tries to pull him away, consequently they get snarled up together, step all over each other, and finally come to a dead standstill in the middle of the room. The girl is very warm and vexed; the little man is warm, too, but quite complacent. He leads her to a seat and stands before her, fanning himself. "You mustn't be so down-hearted," I hear him say; "you really did very nicely for a bud." The girl's face is a study, and she is no longer surprised that girls excuse themselves from dancing with this man, not because of his inefficiency, but because of his conceit.

Ah, what a pleasure it is to turn from such partners to the one who is piloting my little belle. It is the tall, dignified manager. He is a favorite of hers, I think; at least she must enjoy dancing with him. How smoothly they glide about,— the mad diagonal has no fears for them, nor the plunging Sophomore; the bandy-legged man is harder to avoid, because he never continues in the direction he began, and the dignified manager has to put out his left hand to shove him away; still there is no stopping, no bumping; this dancing is indeed the poetry of motion. The manager with glasses is a good dancer, too, but just now you would have cause to doubt it, for his partner, a squarely-built girl with yellow hair and a great number of knife-plaitings, is rather too much of a handicap for him. In the first place she has stretched her hand up onto his shoulder, although he is decidedly tall, and then her arm is outside of his, in a way that pins him down. She seems to have marked out her own course, and evidently does not feel called upon to follow his guidance, so he makes the turn very short and goes off to refresh himself by a polka with the little tomboy. How they fly over the floor; the time is perfect and they are both laughing and chatting.

Her hairpins are raining down and his coat-tails are standing straight out behind. They are having a "splendid time."

"Dear me," says a horrified matron, "that is romping, not dancing; we really ought not to allow the polka."

But why not? It is not the polka that is at fault, for look at this couple. Again it is the little belle, but this time the *blasé* manager is her partner. Indifferent he may be, but when he does dance it is a pleasure to see him. It is like the skimming of a swallow, so swift yet so even. And they are followed by the tall beauty and an equally good partner. No romping there, though it is the polka; no minuette need be more dignified.

Tonight we are to have two Portland Fancies. I am engaged for the first one myself, but that need not prevent my taking mental notes. What a scrambling for places by friends who want to dance in the same set. I am sorry for my little belle, who has gone to the dressing-room "to make everything fast," her partner says, "before starting on the perilous voyage." Why doesn't she hurry; she will surely lose her place? Ah, there she comes, and I needn't have worried. Her friends have been keeping a place for her with jealous care. She takes her stand, supported by the big foot-ball player, and both bow and smile. How delightful it must be to know everyone in the set, I think, as I do the ladies-chain with a girl I never saw before and balance to an unknown corner. We are formed in lines at last, and begin "eight hands round" to the "Mikado" music. I am on the end of our line, and my partner holds me so feebly that I wabble dreadfully and gaze longingly at my pretty belle, who is just coming towards me, firmly held up between her athletic partner and the dignified manager, who is laughing heartily at something she has just said. She nods and smiles at me and says, " Isn't it jolly? " as we pass. I am only a dressing-room acquaintance, but she always speaks to me, though she can't imagine the pleasure it gives to me.

Half around the hall, we meet the little tomboy dancing with the Sophomore, and what a lark they are having. Her hair is half down and she clutches at it whenever she finds a disengaged hand; her train, a very short one, is standing directly out from under her left arm — evidently she does not lace; her corsage bouquet is nothing but stems and hat-pins; she is blowsy and generally dilapidated, but she is pretty and happy and " such fun," that every fourth man she meets asks her to dance the next Portland Fancy with him. She laughs and says she has been engaged for it ever since the last party. And now let us turn our thoughts to supper.

III.

The string of promenaders has grown longer and longer, till now everyone is walking. Directly in front of me is my little belle on the arm of the slender athlete; presently the *blasé* manager joins them. He does not rush across the hall to do so, but stands quietly in the doorway till they come round to him, and then drops into place beside her. He is asking her permission to introduce someone, and I see her shrug her pretty shoulders in a very expressive manner, though she evidently consents, murmurs something to her escort, and they both drop out of the slow moving circle. I am studying her, so take the opportunity to express to my escort a desire to sit down also. He releases my arm with scarcely concealed relief, makes his bow and departs, probably to seek out some friend and relate how he has been "dreadfully stuck on that girl in blue over there." No matter, I am happier now, and I can watch the others much better. Yes; here comes the *blasé* manager with no other than the Superb Being, — "S. B." I call him now, and mentally write it with capitals. He is presented, and after a bow, which is a perfect masterpiece, takes his seat on the bench beside her, sitting well forward, and his whole body turned toward the girl he is addressing. The slender youth with the melancholy eyes does not rise and bow himself away in the usual manner, but merely turns aside, stretches out his legs, crossing one daintily shod foot over the other, shoves his hands deep into his pockets, and letting his head droop forward as well as it can over his high collar, he remains motionless, staring abstractedly into the ever-shifting scene before him. The girl, meantime, leans back, her head resting against the dark green curtain, and answers all questions indifferently, almost disdainfully, as it seems to me. She certainly looks very lovely, but I wish she would be more gracious, for surely this Superb Being is taking special pains to please her, and he is certainly the most perfect creature in the room.

Presently the music sounds again, the slender youth rouses himself, straightens up and draws his hands out of his pockets. The S. B. leans forward still more impressively and asks if he may have the pleasure of a turn, a great condescension on his part, since he seldom dances. The little belle smiles a very superior little smile, though she only says, "I am engaged, thank you," and turns toward the other youth, who is now standing before her. "To you, I suppose?" says the S. B., rising as she rises, and bowing for the first time to the other man, who nods an affirmative; "would you kindly give me half the turn?" he continues.

"It isn't mine to give," answers the slender youth. "Will you then give me the last half of this?" turning again to the waiting damsel. He is evidently not accustomed to pleading, but he does it very gracefully. The little belle is very graceful, too, as she replies quietly, "I have already given it, thank you," making a slight inclination, which indicates the slender youth, who gives her a most eloquent look, and without more delay sweeps her off among the dancers. I feel rather sorry for the S. B., though he squares his shoulders, clasps his hands at the small of his back, and stands looking after the retreating couple with a faintly amused smile curling the corners of his moustache.

And so the evening goes, and it has come to the farewell waltz. I watch my favorites carefully, for I have a feeling that this last waltz has a meaning. The last partner usually conducts a girl to her carriage, and, knowing that this duty will devolve upon him, the sagacious youth generally manages to make it a pleasure as well. I am not disappointed when I see the tall belle with the *blasé* manager, the little tomboy with the jolly Sophomore, the slangy damsel with a flashy youth of doubtful reputation, and so on: the tall manager with the eye-glasses is dancing with a pretty little brown-haired bud, who looks sublimely happy, but the dignified manager is not dancing at all, neither is the slender athlete; both are watching the little belle, who is once more dancing with the big football player. His attentions are really becoming marked, and I find myself wondering (like one of the matrons, who says as much to her neighbor) if there is "anything in it." I have no partner and would like to take an early leave, but cannot because I am going to drive home with another girl; but I can and do seek the dressing-room before the final breaking up, and having got comfortably into my outer wraps, seat myself in a deep window-seat to wait. The last notes have died away, and presently in comes a perfect avalanche of girls, laughing and chattering like so many monkeys.

Such a tossing aside of flowers and scrambling for hoods and party boots, and what a curious mingling of confidences, raptures, and inquiries. "Did you see my hair come down in that last polka?" "Isn't it perfectly lovely?" "Heavens, Mary, you're sitting on my roses." "Mr. B. has asked me for the G.'s German." "Where on earth are my carriage boots?" and so on. The little belle comes to my corner, where her "things" are neatly rolled up in the window-seat. One of the maids follows to assist her, and as the little lady lays down her bouquets, exclaims on their beauty. "Do you like flowers?" asks the little belle, good-naturedly.

"Yes, indeed, Miss; but not like my sister, the lame one,— she loves 'em."

"Oh, have you a lame sister?" This time the voice is very gentle. "Yes, Miss." The little belle picks up the two bouquets again, the roses and the violets; the latter are pretty dilapidated, but the former are still quite bright. "I wonder if you'd like to take her these; they are faded, I know, but many of them will come up in water," and she holds out the superb cluster of "Souvenirs" to the astonished maid, who can hardly express her thanks. My friend is ready to go, and I follow her down the many flights to the entry below. I trust she has someone to look up her carriage, for my last partner bade me good-bye at the dressing-room door. She assures me that someone has gone to find it, and we step back near the stairs, to wait. Down comes my little belle with her attendant cavaliers; the big foot-ball player rushes off to look up her carriage, while the slender athlete takes up his stand beside her in such a way as to shut others off from talking to her. I can hear what he says, and, right or wrong, I mean to listen carefully.

It is about the roses; evidently he had sent them, for after looking at the violets he asks if his could have been more wilted. "No; they were much fresher, so I gave them away."

"Gave them away?"

"Yes; to one of the maids, who had a crippled sister."

"Oh, I see, and you chose to give away my flowers, and keep these?" The tone is slightly constrained, and he looked at her as though waiting for an answer, which comes at last, but almost buried in the violets:

"I gave yours because they were the prettiest, and it seemed to me would give most pleasure."

"Thank you," says the young man, with so much fervor that the commonplace phrase sounds very like love-making, and then both look at each other and smile, and the next minute up comes the big escort to say that he has found the carriage. Everyone calls out "Good night" as she passes, the S. B. goes down the steps with her, together with her other escorts, the dignified manager is already waiting for her at the carriage door; I heard it shut, five or six hats are lifted, there is a chorus of "Good nights," and off she goes. Meantime, I scuttle unescorted after my friend and her cavalier, and am soon lost in the darkness of our joint "booby."

VIOLA.

I WAS a student in the Latin Quarter. I was always impecunious, but during the winter of 1879 I was absolutely poor, too poor to run across the channel for my Christmas plum-pudding,—a degree of poverty which was extreme even in the Latin Quarter.

Early in the spring, to my great joy, word reached me that I had fallen heir to a very comfortable estate; soon after, I moved to twenty something Friedland Avenue, and quite naturally made up in a measure for my pinched existence during the winter by a rather indolent sort of life.

One evening, while I was enjoying a smoke after a good dinner, I was startled by a peculiar sound at my back windows. It was as if somebody were rattling innumerable small shot in a tin can. I went to the window, raised it, and in the uncertain light saw that the noise came from the top flat of the building I was in. I saw that something was being lowered down the side of the house. As I put my head out of the window, a man's voice apologized for the disturbance, assured me that there was no need for alarm, and explained that the noise was made by a fire-escape. Wondering what he could mean, but not interested enough to ask, I withdrew my head.

On the next day I heard the rattling again, and upon looking, saw that the fire-escape consisted of a basket-shaped arrangement, which was lowered by an automatic contrivance of clogs and checks.

The clogs and checks made the rattling sound which had attracted my attention the night before. Impelled by curiosity, I took the trouble to have my noisy neighbor pointed out to me by the concièrge. I found that the man who was so careful to be prepared against flames was a small, active man, with a close featured, perfectly expressionless face. He had dark hair and was clean shaven. His name was Girard Ross.

As I never have sympathy with fire fright I mentally exclaimed, " Poor simpleton," and dismissed the subject from my mind.

I occupied the third floor. On the floor below me was a middle-aged Frenchman, M. Caret, who divided his time between Paris and Geneva, in each of which places he had large jewelry establishments. Shortly after the fire-escape episode, M. Caret decided to give up his rooms, and take up his residence in Geneva permanently. It was with much regret that I found on returning one evening to my rooms a card from him, in which he bade me good-bye, saying he had been called away a week earlier than he had expected. I was very sorry, for M. Caret was a droll old party and the only neighbor I had taken the pains to cultivate.

His rooms were engaged at once by a fine-looking young Frenchman of military bearing, and decidedly distinguished appearance, who, after the first day, spent very little of his time in his rooms and was seldom seen.

Up to that time the man Ross had never spoken to me. A few days after the young Frenchman's appearance, Ross met me in the hallway, begged my pardon, and asked whether M. Caret was apt to be in at that time of day. I replied, I thought not. In my amazement at his addressing me and asking a trivial question, I forgot for the moment that M. Caret had vacated his rooms a week before.

That evening I read till very late. It was long after one when I was ready to stop. As I laid down my book and sat for a moment thinking over its contents, I was startled by an unmistakable groan, deep and horrible. I waited for a few moments, then walked to my door and listened; hearing nothing, I went back to my chair, but I felt troubled. Some twenty minutes must have elapsed when, unable to overcome my uneasiness, I went out into the hallway, and down one flight, for, as nearly as I could tell, the sound had come from the floor beneath me.

As I reached the hall below, the door of what had been M. Caret's reception room opened and a woman's form emerged. Upon seeing me, she started, then rushed towards me.

" Help ! Come ! " she cried, in low, terrified tones, and rushed back into the room.

I followed.

Stretched across a lounge, one hand clutching the edge, his head thrown back, and his eyes staring wide, lay the young Frenchman. He was in evening dress, and a thread of crimson blood trickled down his white shirt front. I hastened over to him ; he was dead, stabbed to the heart.

I turned to the woman at my side. She stood perfectly dazed. After a moment, her face brightened, she became animated as if by a sudden thought, and advancing, said in a firm tone, speaking in French, "I will trust you. This is Count L'Onville. He is a Nihilist; so am I. We were arranging papers this evening. I do not know how long we had been at work. I was leaning over that table" (pointing); "suddenly I was struck from behind. When I recovered, I found the Count as you see. These papers," drawing a package from beneath her cloak, "must not fall into the hands of the police; if they do, I am lost, and many others with me."

Her recital had been cool, methodical, and rapid. As it advanced, I had caught some of her calmness and was soon wrapt in admiration of the speaker before me. Never had I seen such a handsome woman. She was tall and fair, with clear blue eyes and a beautifully poised head. In speaking, she looked straight at the person she was addressing: it was impossible to doubt her sincerity. Her precision and coolness were majestic, but not cruel; it was the effort of a strong will to speak quickly and effectively. As she finished, and glanced at the dead Count, her feminine instinct asserted itself: she shuddered, and with suppressed sobs sank into a chair.

Not a moment did I hesitate; seizing the papers she held in her hand, I rushed noiselessly up to my room, put them in open view on the top of my desk with other papers, and hurried downstairs. I then roused the house and sent for the police.

It never entered my head that the woman I had met in the hallway could be charged with the murder of the Count. She was placed under arrest at once. Her name was Viola Raleigh; she of course refused to tell what her business with the Count had been.

The next afternoon it was discovered that Ross, the occupant of the fourth floor, was not to be found. All the efforts of the detectives to find him were unsuccessful.

Viola Raleigh had no legal aid. I made up my mind to help her. I procured the best criminal lawyer I could, and took him to her. I had no thought of my own danger, my sole object was to help this woman, whom I felt to be innocent, and who had strangely fascinated me. I knew she would sacrifice herself for her cause if necessary. I was right. She refused to tell anything unless I demanded it. Fearful for my own safety, I, of course, did not demand it.

I went away from the jail fully resolved to save her. Her firm determination to protect her cause only added to my admiration for her. My lawyer was completely out of patience, and declared he would have nothing to do with the case. I persuaded him to alter his decision, however. Of course, Ross must be found. Without knowing why, I was sure that he was the murderer. But how to find him? Nobody believed in Viola's innocence but myself; consequently I had overwhelming odds to work against.

I saw her frequently. She seemed utterly regardless of herself, and thought only of her cause. At first I saw, with some mortification, that she did not realize how much I had risked for her, but after a while I noticed a change; she spoke of the risk I was running, and with deep feeling expressed her gratitude again and again. At last she became absolutely uneasy about my position in the matter. One day, just before the trial, she said:

"You will be called upon to tell just what happened on that dreadful night and will have to admit that you know what my business was with the Count, I have been foolish. It will be much better for M. Blanc (the lawyer) to know the whole story."

She spoke in a halting way, very different from her usual clear and fearless style. The same thought was in her mind that flashed into mine the moment I heard her words. She was going to sacrifice her cause for me.

"And are you willing to make this sacrifice?" I asked.

Her eyes dropped and in a low voice she replied: "I am."

On the next day I was unable to see my lawyer, as he had been called out of the city on personal business. I went to see Viola in the afternoon. I found her for the first time greatly excited. A newspaper had published an interview with a man who said he had seen the Count with a picture of a woman which answered to Viola's description. He had noticed the frame particularly. It had a number of rubies around the edge. The implication in this was, of course, only an expression of the opinion held by the public, by the police, by everybody, in fact. The thought until now had not entered Viola's head that I might share the general suspicion.

"You do not believe anything like that, do you?" she asked.

"Of course not," I replied.

After many weary days, during which the police strove hard, but in vain, to convict Viola, she was acquitted for lack of evidence.

Viola's secret had been preserved and she was free. On the day following her release I went to Hotel Splendid, where she had taken rooms. We met in the reception room of the hotel. I urged her to tell me something about herself. The danger was now past, why should she not trust me with her history? Our interview was somewhat constrained on account of the publicity of the place.

She sat toying with a tassel on the arm of her chair. She was greatly agitated; contrary to her usual habit, her eyes were cast down.

"And why," she said slowly and thoughtfully, "should you want to know about me?"

"Do you not know?" I asked. And, lowering my voice, added: "Whoever you are, whatever your history, I love you."

She did not start; raising her eyes to mine, drawing back her beautifully poised head, she made a grand effort at the majestic self-control which had marked her conduct during the investigation. She failed; her mouth twitched convulsively, and the tears welled into her eyes.

"I cannot listen," she murmured, and hastily left me.

I went home in a very troubled state of mind. She had become more interested in herself because I had become interested in her. I knew her strong will, and knew that if she felt it her duty to turn a deaf ear to me, she would do so. And yet she loved me — there was no mistaking that.

On my way to Avenue Friedland I met my lawyer, who had been to my rooms.

"Have you heard?" he asked.

"No," I replied. "What?"

"Why, they have caught Ross. They have found bills upon him which have been identified by a friend of the Count's as bills he gave to the Count in payment of a bet, the Saturday before the murder."

I went to my rooms, musing. Suddenly the whole thing came to me like a flash. I connected several circumstances which had seemed to be of little importance before. I remembered that M. Caret's departure was unexpected. I remembered my meeting with Ross in the hallway, and, last of all, I remembered Ross's "fire-escape." His crazy notion about fire was madness with a method. Ross had intended to secure M. Caret's diamonds. Finding his victim gone, he had robbed the Count. I shuddered as I thought how the villain, lowering himself by means of his fire-escape, had probably peered into my room again and again — I might have been his victim.

I arrived at my rooms in Avenue Friedland. As I entered, I saw a letter on my table. It had arrived by the morning post, but in my excitement I had failed to read it before leaving the house. I opened it now. It was a card, dated the afternoon before, and must have been written immediately after I had left Hotel Splendid; it read as follows:

I love you too well to stay.   Open the package of papers.
Did you know what she suffers you would partly forgive
                                                    VIOLA.

I rushed to my desk.   I seized the papers I had received from Viola on the night of the murder.   I tore the package open.   As I did so, a tiny, gold-handled dagger dropped out, and stuck, quivering, in the desk, followed by a miniature in a gold frame set with rubies.   I looked; it was Viola.

With feverish haste I clutched the papers before me and read.   .   .   .   They were love letters from the Count.

Ross succeeded in proving an alibi.

The murder of the Count L'Onville remained a mystery to the world.

A. A. Gardner, '87.

A HOLLOW SHAM.

IT was a cold, dreary September and yet it was my two weeks' vacation. Already a week had gone by and my wife and I had not decided where to go. Our choice certainly was limited, for my salary was not stupendous, and to every place that was mentioned there seemed to be some objection. The chief literature to be found in our parlor was guide-books,— blue, red, yellow, star-spangled, straggly-mapped guide-books. But no place within our means seemed to suit. Several times we had decided on a beautifully described country hotel, when my wife would discover that either " good drainage " was not mentioned in the advertisements, or else some other trifle interfered. I had lounged about the house until I was tired of doing nothing. I had gone down to the post-office for every single mail. I had carried letters down one by one so as to take up time. I had sat on the steps and talked with my next-door neighbor until I hated the sight of him. Finally I grew desperate. My vacation was slipping away, and we had not yet found any place in which to spend it.

It was Friday night when, on going into the parlor, I found my wife seated at a table which was covered with rows of figures and all kinds of time-table hieroglyphics.

"What are you trying to do?" I cried.

"Why," she said, " I'm trying to find out how to get to Blankboro. Here is one train which gets there, but which never starts. These time-tables are so puzzling. Now here is the 11.02 for Blankboro, which only goes to Z—— one day, and then continues on the next day,—a sort of serial train."

"Oh, no," I said; "a freight train loaded with grain would be a cereal train"—

She paid no notice, but went on, "Then here is the 9.05 which gets to Blankboro at 8.03 (*before it started*), and I cannot understand that; unless the sign * explains it, for * means 'mixed train.' It is mixed. The 5.05 says ‡, which is 'daily except Monday.' Does that mean that it runs hourly on Monday? This train, too, arrives at Axboro and then leaves from a station two or three down in the list. I have drawn about ten diagrams, and I cannot make it clear."

I took hold of the thing, and when I had finished it was settled that we were to go to Blankboro on the 3.35 train. Blankboro, I found out from Maria, was a place on the sea-shore, about forty miles from the city, where there was a quiet hotel, "pleasant literary company, beautiful drives, fine croquet grounds, hops twice a week, and board $8 a week including soap and candles." Whether it was the "literary," or the croquet, or the free soap, that attracted Maria, I do not know.

On Tuesday we started, and, to my disgust, it was another disagreeable day,—a day that reminded you that October was creeping upon September with her chilly, cold rains.

"Are you sure that this car goes to Blankboro?" asked Maria, when we were seated, and all the bundles bestowed in the rack.

"No; I am not. You cannot be sure of anything in this life," I answered.

"Don't you think you had better ask the conductor if this is the right car?" she persisted.

"No," I said.

Finally, after fidgeting around and disturbing my attention from my newspaper, she leaned forward and asked the gentleman in front if this car went to Blankboro.

"What?" he said.

She repeated her question once, and then twice. Finally the man said he did not know. By this time the whole car was looking at us. The train was a very accommodating train and went very slowly, stopping at every man's back door. There was nothing to look at outside, and the people in the car were terribly uninteresting. To be sure, the train boy had been through about seventeen times, leaving boxes of archæological candy, nice little infantile picture-books, illustrated papers with enlivening detailed pictures of the execution of a noted murderer. I had read all I could of the comic paper before he came round to collect. I had nearly twisted my head off trying to incorporate within me in as quick a time as possible the contents of the paper whose leaves were not cut. I had tried to get some amusement out of the "Notice to Passengers." At last

"I wonder how long it takes to arrive at Blankboro?" I remarked.

"I don't know," Maria said. "Won't you ask that brakeman?"

"Do you think I am an Interrogation Point?" I replied, and I settled down to try and take a nap. Suddenly it struck me that we were stopping an unconscionably long time at this station. Maria at last poked me and said:

"Won't you go and see what the matter is?"

The rain was coming down hard as ever and it was beginning to grow dark. I looked out of the window, and saw a little dingy shed situated in the midst of a great, flat, muddy plain. I jumped up and looked around; we were the sole occupants of the car.

"Where are all the passengers?" I cried.

"I saw them getting out some time ago, and I wanted to get you to ask them where they were going," said Maria.

I dashed out of the door and upon the platform. There was no car in front of us,— nothing but the long line of track stretching on through the desolate country. A forest fire had just gone over the place, and it was a vast wilderness of blackened stumps and pools of dirty water. I rushed for the shed which apparently was the station, and I met the station master coming out with a lantern. He had just locked up and was going home. When he saw me with my glaring face, and Maria poking her head out of the car window, regardless of the rain, he let his lantern fall in amazement.

"What do you mean," I cried, "by dropping cars around loose in this manner; and where is this hole?"

"Well, young feller, cool down," the man said. "Do you think I'm an encyclopædia? I didn't uncouple this car and I can't tell you anything about it," and he was walking off when I stopped him and asked him what we were going to do.

"Anything you like," he said.

"But we cannot sit out here on this platform all night," I cried.

"Well, yer might get Hansom to take yer down to the hotel," and he pointed to an old tumble-down barn across the road. I walked over to it and discovered a man sitting in the remains of an old carry-all, smoking a pipe.

"Look here," I cried, "can you take me down to the hotel?"

The man lazily opened one eye and without removing his pipe, murmured, "I can." I waited a little while, and then, getting exasperated, said:

"Well, will you?"

He looked at me for a few minutes and then walked off. I ran after him, when he suddenly stopped and called out, "Mary Susan, will I take a party over to the hotel?" Then somebody called out, "Wal, I s'pose you'll hev to, but don't make the mare go faster than a walk. Yer know she's pretty heevy."

In the course of half an hour we got into the tobacco-scented, dilapidated vehicle, and the mare walked solemnly out into the mud and rain. A more forsaken spot I could not imagine.

"Whatever possessed anybody to build a town here?" I asked.

"The Lord only knows; I don't," the driver mumbled; "there's no excuse for its existence."

The only thing that relieved the dreariness of the ride was a gorgeous sign on a little shanty, "Elite Shaving Parlors." Even this could hardly evoke a smile. We drove on and on, over a perfectly flat country, covered everywhere with charred stumps.

At last the salt smell announced that we were approaching the sea. I looked out through the little mud-stained window and saw not far off an immense, barn-like structure with several rows of windows. It had no blinds; the paint had long ago washed off; the grass was growing in all the driveways; the piazzas had broken down.

"Here we are," the driver said; "five dollars, please."

"What! five dollars to take a person to this God-forsaken place?"

"Wal, yer see, we don't very often get a chance ter bring anyone here." He had hardly ceased speaking when suddenly three men with guns appeared right in front of the carriage. My wife screamed, and then, recovering herself, wanted me to ask them what they wanted. They held a parley with the driver, and finally, after many gesticulations and queer looks, we were set down, and our unique conveyance tottered off back to the village. We entered the hotel by what seemed to be the back door. I went up to the desk to sign my name. There seemed to be no head clerk, but three men and two women were sitting behind the counter playing poker. "Bring the register, Bill," one of them said.

"The cook used it for kindling," Bill said.

I looked at them in amazement. "Well," I said, "at what hour will supper be ready?"

"Hy, Bill, don't you 'ear the gent a-hasking when we hare going to 'eave on the victuals?"

"Tell his blokes, when we hare ready," the other replied.

I turned away. "Take the fust room yer find empty and make yerself ter hum," one of the women called out.

My wife and I wandered up the corridor until we found a room which suited. "Are we in a lunatic asylum?" Maria asked.

I was too mad and tired and wet and hungry to answer rationally. I sat and glared at her.

"Say, this is a gay old vacation," at last I said.

Maria said nothing, but took a pack of cards out of her pocket and began playing solitaire on the bed. I got up and looked out of the window. The hotel was situated on a bluff overlooking the dreary expanse of stormy waters. Not a tree was in sight. Nothing but the fog and the gloomy gray of the sky and storm.

Not long afterwards, we heard a gong boom out through the house. We went down into the dining-room and found a pile of eatables at one end of the room on a table. Everybody was making a rush for this, and carrying off as much as he could procure.

Driven by hunger, we were compelled to do the same. All the evening there was the most horrible noise in the halls, and the shouting and singing continued all night. In the morning the same disorder appeared. It was still raining hard and blowing violently. The rain had leaked into our room, and, as it was too wet to stay there, I went downstairs. Most of the servants and clerks appeared to be drunk. I went into the billiard room. There was a peripatetic table there with four wobbling legs; the cloth was torn as if a reaping machine had been over it. My wife and I, however, managed to start a little game, when we were suddenly interrupted by two billiard balls whizzing past our heads. I ran to the door and saw the head clerk rushing up the stairs. "Thatsh only a joke," he cried. I did not attempt to argue with him, but took my wife's arm and went up into the reading-room. I was just engaged in reading a two-weeks-old paper when we were startled by a noise outside of trampling and shouting. Soon someone in the house ran down the entry crying, "To arms." I looked out of the window and saw a party of men hammering at the door. Then two men from the house went out the back way with guns and approached them. I listened carefully to what they said. I soon understood all. The owner of this hotel had not paid the servants their wages. They had turned him out, and were now running the hotel by themselves.

The party of men just arrived were the sheriff, the owner of the hotel, and their followers, who were trying to recover the property. Suddenly I saw the men from the house come back, and I heard the door bolted. Then came a crash, a sound of broken glass, and I saw the whole ten men piling rapidly in through the window.

Screams and oaths resounded up the corridors. "Guard the doors!" I heard one man shout. Then before I could explain to Maria what it was all about, three men rushed into our room, and, despite our struggles, carried us downstairs. We found the sheriff there with all the servants in charge. I attempted to explain that I was a boarder and not a servant. "That makes no difference," he said; "I shall detain you as a witness."

I shall not attempt to describe the next three days, during which we were kept in custody in that bleak hotel. It is enough to say that on the fourth day, after having testified with heartfelt pleasure against the servants, we were released, paid six dollars apiece, and allowed to take the train for Boston.

Our old driver drove us down to the station, and I thought I saw a dim smile flicker for a moment in his half-closed eyes when he said, " Did yer have a real jolly time down to the hotel ? "

It was Saturday night when we returned to the city. I went back to work on Monday morning. My vacation had hardly been what you would call a success.

Charles Warren, '89·

IN THE REDWOODS.

IT was midnight of November 25th, 1880. The moon, half spent, rose over the long, unbroken range of mountains which extend along the northern coast of California from the Bodega Inlet to Humboldt Bay. Perhaps an hour before midnight, a young girl stood in the doorway of a deserted cabin, far up in the Russian River cañon, watching the east grow light and waiting for the moon to rise. A trail, half obliterated by the growth of scrub pines and fallen trees, ran a few yards in front of the cabin, and led on down the cañon to an old logging camp. By the light of the moon this trail would be plainly visible at a place a quarter of a mile higher up the mountain, where it crossed a clearing in the redwoods, and toward this spot the girl's face was turned. She was alone, and seemed impatient for the coming light which lingered so long among the tall trees on the summit of the range. A cloak, black and long, and from its shape evidently a "gentleman's," was thrown over her shoulders and its hood covered her head. There was no sound to stir the deep stillness of the forest, save now and then the cry of some mountain cat — and she had played with mountain cats, why should they frighten her? Yet she shuddered at the cry, it was so near, and even the creaking of a board as she stepped back a little into the cabin startled her. "My," she said to herself, "how scared I am at nothin'." Then she drew the cloak closer about her and stepped out.

The moon was rising. It looked like a great fire among the redwoods before it came up from their midst, but when it had finally risen, all the cañon was flooded with its light. The trail which Mal had been straining her eyes to see through the darkness, now showed clearly where it came from a thick growth of chaparell, and she watched its stretch across the clearing more earnestly than ever. She had not long to watch, for soon he for whom she was waiting issued from the bush. He was on horseback, and a riderless horse followed him. At the centre of the clearing he stopped and discharged a small revolver. Mal's heart leaped. "All is right, all is right," she said slowly to herself; but her conscience told her all was wrong, and she burst into sobs.

"Poor Dad, poor Dad, he'll never take me back,— en Ben, en Jim. Oh, I know he'll never do it. But if he should not," she said between her teeth — "I've seen folks die, en, en"— but a pair of strong arms were around her, and that voice which had led her so far on was calling her his Mal, his sweet Mal, his little Mal, and asking her if tears were all she had for him.

Then her arms sought his neck, and she begged him not to be angry with her. "I won't cry no more," she said imploringly, and would not unclasp his neck until he had promised never to be angry with her again.

"And now, Mal," he said, "we must be getting out of here. We'll cross the river and stop at Jim's."

"No, no, no," she begged. "Not at Jim's; Jim knows me. Jim would know something was wrong,— en, en, he might kill you," she whispered, "if he happened to think that you were taking me away."

"O Mal, why do you always think of some such horrid thing as killing? But, if you can stand it, we'll cross the range and stop in one of the old logging camps tonight, and tomorrow go on to Sonoma, where we can take the cars."

"Oh, I can stand it," she said earnestly. "I've been there with Dad lots o' times; only please don't stop at Jim's."

"Well, we won't, since it troubles you, my love,— but do you know, Mal," he continued, "you look divine in that coat of mine. I shall have to will it to you," he said with a little laugh. It was a forced laugh, but it was just as sweet to Mal, and when he lifted her into the saddle, she clung to his neck until he had kissed her many times, and called her over and over again by all those sweet names which love makes up for its ornaments. Then he threw himself into his own saddle, and in single file, he leading, down into the depths of the cañon they departed.

The trail which they followed had once been used as a log-way. On each side rose the giant redwoods, towering high and dark above them. In the dense part of the forest, where the moon only shone on the higher branches of the trees, they seemed like gray-crested phantoms; and the scrubs about their base, stirred by the light wind, seemed to breathe a sigh as Mal passed beneath them; and Mal answered them with a sigh from her own heart.

Among these trees had been her home; their every sound and look, in pleasant and fearful weather, she knew; and now she was leaving them,— was it forever?

Shortly they came to the old logging camp where she had spent so many happy hours watching the huge logs thin themselves out into lumber, and seeing the great saw spin round and round. Perhaps some of that very lumber which she had seen cut had gone to the city to help build his house, the house which he had told her was to be hers. Thus she thought on until, leaving the camp behind, they descended into the creek-bed and followed on down towards the river, which they could hear rippling over the stones at the crossing. The river crossed, they left the trail and made a wide detour to avoid passing Jim's. It was so strange, she thought, to go by Jim's without stopping; Jim, who had rescued her from drowning when she had attempted to cross the river to his cabin during the rising of the river the fall before; Jim, who was almost as dear as her own father, and so much gentler; Jim, who loved her so.

"Jim!" she called aloud before she knew what she had said.

Her lover halted, startled at the sudden cry, and came to her.

"I didn't mean to do that," she said, "it came out,— I couldn't help it. I was thinking so much of him, and wishing I might just say good-bye to him, that it slipped out all of a suddint."

A mile beyond Jim's they came into the trail again, just where it commences its upward climb into the redwoods of the coast range, and an hour later, at the edge of the woods of El Diablo, they came upon the cabin where they were to spend the night. Here they dismounted, and Mal's lover led the horses into the brush, while she, not the least afraid, pushed open the door into the dark and vacant hut.

There was a close and stifling odor within, from the old and musty straw scattered over the bunk in the corner. A wildcat pushed by Mal, and with a low growl jumped out through the window. She gave a little start. "Jip's here yet," she said, referring to the late occupant of the shanty; "Jip knows what's nice." She sat down on the edge of the rude bunk and looked out to the brush, where she could see her lover loosening the girths of the saddles. Then she once more thought of her home far back at the head of the Russian River; that dear old river; how she hated to leave its soft ripple and its blue, clear waters; and her "Dad," and "Jim," and her brothers; thoughts of them all came surging up from her heart. She hid her face in her hands and burst into sobs. So long as he was with her she was happy; but alone, how timid she grew.

Some stakes had been torn from the roof of the cabin, and through the opening a little moonlight fell upon her. When she raised her face it was very white. The hood had fallen partially from her head, and one of her locks of ruddy hair had shaken itself loose from the knot into which it had been tied and had fallen down upon her shoulder. Her lover kissed her when he came. Then all was changed, and her heart leaped with joy.

"You are not sorry, my sweet one, you came, are you?" he said tenderly to her.

"No," she sobbed, and looked up at him. "Why do you always think I am sorry? I ain't sorry,— only Dad,— Dad will miss me, and I know he'll never take me back; en Jim. Jim will miss me, too." She could say no more for her sobs.

"Ah, my little one, I am afraid you are getting tired of my love instead of I —"

"No, no, no, I'm not, I'm not. I won't speak of them again; I won't, I won't," she cried, clinging closer to him and trying to stop the heavy sobs which would come, even when he had told her all over again how much she was to him.

"En you'll marry me when we get to the city, won't you?" she asked, looking up into his face.

But he turned his head away, and she could not see the look which came into his face; so the tears and sobs came back to her again, and he had to comfort her with his words.

"My dear Mal, why do you cry so? There, there, you are tired. Let me kiss them away! Why, Mal, my love, do not cry! You know I love you, my sweet one. There, rest your head here and try to sleep; I will waken you when it is light." So with a sigh, her head dropped upon his shoulder, and Mal had gone to sleep.

The moon has risen a little higher. It shone full upon Mal's face, and her lover kissed her. "One would almost take her for a man in this coat of mine," he said to himself; "but how sweet her face is"; and another caress told him how sweet, indeed, it was.

A cool breeze had sprung up from the coast, and was bringing a heavy fog with it. For some time Mal's lover watched it, through a break in the trees, come rolling in over the range and settle down in a cloud over the Russian River Valley. Then he must have fallen asleep; but only for a moment. He awoke with a little start, and under the impression that he had heard voices. He listened. The wind was stirring the dead leaves outside, and moaning among the pines. Was it only the wind he had heard? Gently he laid Mal down upon the bunk and drew the hood over her face. He stepped to the window and listened again. Still there was only the sound of the wind among the trees. Yet he was sure he had heard other sounds than those of the forest. Yes, he was right. Presently there came the sound as of crackling brush. Someone was coming. Yes, now he caught a glimpse of some half-dozen horsemen on the trail. "God! Her father's horse and Jim's," he breathed; "they're after me; they'll lynch me if they catch me." He glanced hastily at Mal, kissed her softly,— it must be his last, he knew,— then out through the door, into the chaparell, onto his horse, and away.

The men coming up the trail heard his horse crash through the brush in the distance, but thought it some fleeing deer startled at their approach.

A little before the cabin the men halted and dismounted. Their leader was Mal's father. He went softly to the window and looked in. The figure in the black coat caught his eye. He thought it the abductor of his child, and the thought fired him. It was all he cared for; to have his vengeance upon

him.   He did not look to see if Mal was there, too.
He did not think of her.   His passion for revenge
had mastered him.   He beckoned to the rest.

" Mind, boys, don't let him hollar.   Muffle him
with the sack and tie his feet fast."   It was quietly
done.   The moon hid itself behind some dark
clouds.   The foggy wind sobbing among the redwoods ceased, and all the voices of the deep forest
were hushed.

By the sound of a distant whistle they knew it
was nearing morning.   " Ye know the tree, boys,—
up with the rietta, and give me first hand on the
rope, if you please."

There was a sound as of a rope running over
hard bark.   Something dark rose a few feet into
the air and stopped.   A tremor passed through the
figure, it twitched convulsively.   The leafless bough
from which it hung swayed up and down for a
moment.   Then all grew still save the giant tree,
which moaned and moaned and knew no resting.

It was morning — but in the woods of El Diablo
all was dark as night.   The wind was springing up
afresh and the white, damp fog grew thicker and
thicker as it stole in among the tall redwoods like
a phantom, obliterating all before it.   Like a shroud
for the dead it came and wrapped its mantle of
white about the figure which swayed to and fro in
the morning wind, while a voice born of the heart
of El Diablo, in the depth of the redwoods, moaned
the name of Mal.

Case Bull, '92·

OLD man Town lay on his death-bed. His head, with its white hair, and its rough, unshaven face sunk into pale hollows, lay quite motionless on the pillow. His arms and hands, once so brawny, rested thin and weak on the dark coverlet, which was barely stirred with his labored breathing. For many years, ever since he had first been able to handle a jack-knife, Marcus Town had been studying the problem of perpetual motion, in theory and practice; and on his bed now, just within his reach, lay a simple combination of wheels and springs, to which his last conscious moments had been devoted.

Sam, the younger of two sons, but himself with grizzled head, was the only watcher. He sat in a stiff, straight-backed chair, close by the narrow bed, nursing one leg with his large, long, bony hands. He sat still, but his eyes wandered restlessly about, glancing now and then at the pale figure on the bed, but turning quickly away, with an expression of pain, to the smoky ceiling, or the rag-carpet on the floor, or out of the small, dust-covered panes of the narrow window to the fields and hills and woods of the farm, which lay sleeping in the warm afternoon sunlight. The usual apparatus of the sick-room was missing here — no half-emptied bottles with sinister-looking contents, no dreary array of spoons and goblets. The most accessible physician had once spoken contemptuously of perpetual motion; and Marcus Town had sworn long since that his enemy should not be allowed to help him out of the world.   Sam had pleaded again and again to be permitted to fetch some doctor, but his father insisted that he could die without assistance.   Women the old gentleman would not have about him anyway, and Sam's wife, the only woman on the place, dared not show her face inside the door.   His father had always slighted Sam, because he had no head for machinery; but it was Sam who alone thought it worth while to watch by the dying old man.   His brother Barnard had inherited all his father's passion for perpetual motion; there was just one thing lacking about his latest device, and, afraid lest his father should complete the machine before he did, he was hard at work now at his own wheels, in the workshop close at hand.   So Sam sat alone with his dying father.

The sudden sound of Barnard's hammer startled the sick man, and the white head rose from the pillow.   The eyes opened slowly and glanced wearily about.   As they fell on the gear that lay on the bed at his side, a flash of light came into them.   The old man started up and grasped the wheels, but his strength failed him and he fell back with a groan.   Sam had risen anxiously and now bent over the bed.   The painful breathing and the little flutter of the heart showed that life was not yet out; and, somewhat reassured, Sam sat down again, stopping, however, to pick up the little machine and put it back within the old man's reach.   He handled it carefully, and after he had seated himself, he eyed it wistfully.   Sam had never lost faith that his father or his brother would sometime astonish the world with perpetual motion;

but he could not help thinking now of the place which those bits of iron had held in his father's heart to the exclusion of all besides; and he almost wished that it had been given to someone outside his family to electrify the world. He did not regret his own burden — it was no sacrifice to him to carry on the farm alone — but it had been hard to be shut out from the sympathy of his father and brother.

Barnard's hammer again broke in on his revery; he turned uneasily toward the bed as he heard it. His father's head moved mechanically from side to side once or twice: and then the old man rose slowly in his bed until he sat upright, his eyes rolling wildly about. Sam sprang to his feet, and as he approached the bedside, his father reached out convulsively and grasped his arm. The pale lips began to move, almost inaudibly at first. But the voice grew more and more clear and distinct as he went on. Sam was bewildered; the strange light in his father's eyes frightened him. The old man was talking about wheels and springs; he knew now; he had found the only thing lacking to make his machine perfect, the thing he had been struggling for for years,— so much was clear, but poor Sam could understand no more. He shouted to Barnard, but the sound of Barnard's hammer rose and drowned his voice. The dying man had clutched his arm with a grasp that he could not shake off. He bent his whole mind on what the old man was repeating over and over again: but just as there began gradually to dawn on his consciousness the meaning of the words, the voice sank to a whisper, and the white head fell back on the pillow.

C. W. Willard.

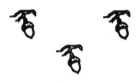

A STREAK OF CRIMSON.

HE was a Senior, and he stood before the glass in his chamber up in Beck, shaving. He was one of the few men in Beck Hall who did shave themselves always, and because he had just cut himself terribly across the cheek was no sign that he was a novice at the art. His language, when the blood showed itself and several drops of crimson ran down his cheek, was not at all mild; and it showed, also, that a cut was a very uncommon thing. He tried to wipe away the blood; he tried brown paper, but the pieces he put on the wound seemed to melt away and float down his cheek; he tried other useless things; and then in his desperation he used a big piece of court-plaster. That had the desired effect and he went on shaving.

" On Class Day, too," he said to himself between his teeth as he daubed his chin and mouth with lather. " The first time this year," and he stopped to wipe his razor on a bit of paper; " that's what comes from shaving yourself,— and on Class Day, too," and again he was emphatic.

Alfred Miles was not a profane man always. He had no hesitation about using pretty strong English when the occasion demanded. He used unconventionally warm words when his " goody " made his bed and forgot to put on any sheets, or when she reversed the position of his head, turning down the sheets at the foot of his bed and tucking them in at

the head.   That was a particular trick of the
"goodies" of Beck, and Miles thought it no more
than right that it should be condemned.   But when
he cut himself across the cheek, and on the morning of Class Day, the limited vocabulary of the
wicked was most terribly strained.   Every time he
passed before a mirror, and he had many in his
room, his room-mate was impressed with Miles' misfortune, not so much from the 'cut itself as from the
force and clearness of the arguments he set forth
proclaiming his ill luck.

"And on Class Day, too,— Class Day above all
other days. *My* Class Day"; and then he digressed
into other stronger arguments.

It was perfectly natural that Miles should feel
badly over the disfigurement of his face on this day,
above all others, when he hoped to look his best.
He was not only a Senior, but he was a very prominent one, and much was expected of him in a classical as well as a social capacity.   The classical would
have gone all well enough with a cut such as
he had given himself, and likewise the social,
had it not been for something which he would
have been very loath to admit had he been accused
of it.

The truth of this statement was fully apparent to
Boler, Miles' Freshman room-mate, when he tried to
condole with the Senior by saying:

"It don't look badly, Milesey; anyhow *she* won't
mind."

Miles threw a book at his sympathizer and said
cuttingly:

"You Freshman!"

Nevertheless, he had to smile in spite of himself at his room-mate's remark, and went to the glass to see if the cut did look so *very* badly.

It was a pretty bad cut, the worst he had ever given himself. But for some unaccountable reason, perhaps the Freshman's remark, he said no more about it; only now and then he went to the glass and examined his face carefully.

She was a perfect study on the afternoon of Class Day, a study of life and motion, a harmony of color, a dream of loveliness; and as they passed through the college yard, she with Mr. Alfred Miles and another lady with Boler, her appearance was the cause of many conjectures as to who she was.

A group of men they passed, who knew Miles, lifted their hats wonderingly and turned their heads to follow her with their eyes.

"Who is that with Miles?" asked one. The rest shrugged their shoulders. "Awfully swell," continued the speaker, "whoever she is."

And he was right.

She was tall, rather slender, and she moved with a grace which, though perfectly natural, never failed to attract attention. And the attention once attracted to her, seldom cared to hurry to others. She was neither a blonde nor a brunette, wholly; she had some of the charms of each. Her hair was light, and would have curled had she cared to have it so, but she preferred to wear it after a style of her own, — a sort of loose knot. Her face was not simply pretty; it was more. It bore an expression of refinement and sympathy difficult to describe, while her blue eyes put the life and spirit into what she said, and her voice was as sincere and sweet as one could wish in a person who was really human. And Helen Rove was surely that. It was one of her chief charms, her realness; and withal she was as full of fun as ever a girl could be.

Now, as she walked across the yard, by the side of Miles, she ran on with some light talk, using her eyes and her smiles as well as her tongue to make her companion understand how happy she was. And she felt her happiness as well as looked it. It was her first Class Day.

They were going to the Alpha Delta Phi spread in the Hemenway Gymnasium. At the door Miles showed his tickets and they passed in to join the throng already there. The orchestra was playing a merry galop as they entered, and Miles advised Boler and Mrs. Longwood, Helen's aunt, whom the Freshman was accompanying, to find seats in the gallery, while he with Helen pushed a way through the rows of wallflowers, out onto the floor, and took up the lively step of the dance.

From the balcony Boler and Mrs. Longwood could see the dancers on the floor below very distinctly. The dress Helen wore made her easily distinguishable even to her aunt, who was exceedingly near-sighted, but who strenuously refused to put on glasses until, as she said, she had given up trying to be young.

Boler was making himself very entertaining.

" Have you noticed what a terrible cut Miles has on his face?" he said, turning to Mrs. Longwood. "He got it shaving himself this morning," he continued, not waiting for an answer, "and I thought it would almost spoil his Class Day. He wanted to look so fine, you know, on Class Day, because he's a Senior, and because,"— he hesitated,— "because he has so much to do, you know, today."

"How dreadful," replied Mrs. Longwood. "I did notice it. I should think he would have felt terribly; but aren't you afraid he is giving too much time to Helen? I know he has so much to do."

"O pshaw! no, Mrs. Longwood, he couldn't give too much time to *her*," Boler said, gallantly, thinking that he had undoubtedly scored a point on his exalted room-mate.

Nevertheless, Mrs. Longwood was a bit nervous and insisted that Boler should go and find Miles and relieve him of Helen.

But Boler, though he was a Freshman, and though he bore the memory of a shock he had received that morning by coming in contact with a flying book, had no intentions of doing anything to disturb his room-mate's plans. Those plans had been more or less definitely arranged between the two men beforehand, and Boler understood very well that what Miles wanted of him was to look after Helen's aunt. He knew more than this. He knew that Miles and Helen were in love; Miles had as much as told him so; he suspected them engaged; if they weren't he knew they would be before Class Day was over, if he, Boler, did as he should and as Miles expected him to do. And so, with a sort of fellow-feeling which even a Freshman, it must be admitted, has for a Senior,— a feeling one has for any person whom some day he hopes to equal,— Boler played his cards the best he knew how.

So it was that he was unable to find Miles to relieve him of Helen. He told Mrs. Longwood they had probably gone over to Memorial Hall to try the music there. But the two were not to be found at Memorial, and Mrs. Longwood grew quite uneasy.

"Where do you suppose they can have gone?" she asked.

"Around to some of the private spreads, probably," Boler said, carelessly; "but don't worry, Mrs. Longwood, they are bound to turn up before it is time to go to the Tree. It's quite the custom, you know, for Seniors to go alone with young ladies on Class Day; and if you don't mind we'll go back to the room and wait for them there. Miles has to come up to change his clothes before Tree time, you know. We'll be surer to find them there, in the room, I think, than most any other place."

Although the celebrations about the Tree were to be at five o'clock, Miles and Helen did not reach the rooms in Beck much before that hour.

Boler had nearly exhausted himself in trying to entertain Mrs. Longwood, who seemed to grow more and more nervous as the time neared five; and he felt very much relieved when he saw Miss Rove come in with Miles.

She was radiant. Her face was aglow with color, her eyes sparkled with merriment, her voice was a ripple of laughter. Her hair had become quite disordered, and curls crept out from beneath her hat and fell in places they were not meant to be. She tried to tell her aunt, in one breath, everything she had been doing in the last two hours. They had been here and they had been there, to so many spreads, and she had had *such* a good time, and she had danced so much, and O no, she wasn't a bit tired, not the least bit. It was very pleasant to hear her run on in this way. A girl at Harvard, so enthusiastic, was a strange sight.

In the meantime Miles was getting himself into his oldest clothes, preparatory to going to the Tree. When he came out he was a perfect sight. He had on an old pair of knickerbockers, heavy tan shoes, an old sweater, which had once been white, and a red and white cap. The cut on his face was showing signs of renewed activity, and it was with some difficulty that a piece of new court-plaster was made to adhere to the wound.

Once ready, however, he left Helen and her aunt in charge of Boler, who was to escort them to the Tree, and hastened to join the crowd of Seniors which was gathering in the yard, preparatory to marching to the quadrangle about the old Elm.

It was a sight Helen Rove never forgot.

The rows of seats, tier upon tier, which occupied three sides of the quadrangle, were one mass of color and life. The varied summer shades of the dresses of the girls, the gaudy and white parasols they carried, the flowers they wore, and, above all, their smiling, happy faces, made a background beautiful beyond description for the stretch of green lawn upon which, seated in a semi-circle about the Tree, were the hundreds of students.

She could liken the scene only to a huge bouquet. Everything seemed to be color and life. The Tree itself wore a garland of roses; and when the shouting began, for the athletic teams, for the professors, for the buildings, for old Harvard, one class for another, and all once again for old Harvard, Helen Rove could scarcely keep from 'rahing, too. But when the Seniors made their grand rush for the flowers which decked the old Elm, she fairly rose from her seat in her excitement at the scene before her,— or was it because Miles had fought his way to the front, and now, clambering over the shoulders of his classmates, was snatching a huge handful of roses from the prized wreath?

"The old thing's bleeding yet," Miles said to himself as he stood before the glass in his chamber that evening, examining the cut on his face. He was through cursing his luck, he was through crying over spilt milk; and although the blood came quite freely when he washed the dust and dirt of the Tree scrimmage from his face, he expressed only a mild sort of regret at his misfortune, and said to the cut, "Well, bleed if you want to."

It took him some time to prepare for the evening festivities. He couldn't seem to get a collar that just suited him, and even when he had finally selected one, and had broken one of his polished finger-nails in trying to button it, a drop of crimson blood stole down his cheek and fell on the white linen.

Well, then his patience and his temper completely slipped from his control, and he said what he thought and felt very forcibly, and so loud were his words that Boler came in from the next room to warn him.

"They couldn't hear it, could they?" Miles asked, alarmed at the thought that Helen might have heard his language.

"She could, I think," replied the Freshman, sarcastically, "for she asked if you were in the habit of talking to yourself. I said I guessed you were reciting one of your impromptu speeches; but you had better be careful," and Boler vanished behind the portières and closed the door.

Miles came out later, quite a different looking object than he had gone in. He was in evening dress and in every particular was most correct. He had powdered the cut on his face so that it showed scarcely at all. He was very much at ease.

Helen was sitting in the window-seat by the open window. Heavy portières fell at her side and there were pillows at the back. It was evening and growing dark. In the room the lights had not been lit. Across the sea of green-leaved elms in the college yard she could see the western sky, a glory of splendid colors. Slowly the brighter colors faded away. A new and timid moon shone out in the cooling sky, like a diamond crescent on the fair breast of a woman.

Mrs. Longwood was resting in Boler's chamber. Boler himself had gone to dinner. Helen was alone. Miles saw her there in the window-seat as he entered, and he was quiet that he might not disturb her. Softly he parted the portières at her head and leaning over touched his lips to her hair.

She gave a sudden little start and looked up.

"Oh!" she said, trembling, "you frightened me so."

"Frightened you?" he asked.

"Yes, frightened me," she replied, slowly; rather severely.

"I am sorry," he said; "sorry, too, that you should be indignant, and I half believe you are."

"I am — indignant," she faltered; but her "am" was the woman's "no" that meant "yes," and Miles knew it, and threw his arms about her, half smothering her with his caresses.

"You mustn't, you mustn't. O Allie, you mustn't," she said, and tried to mean it.

"And who's a better right, Helen?" he asked, as if hurt at what she had said.

She couldn't answer him that; but her face and her beautiful eyes told him better than words ever could that there was no one. And so there they sat together, before the open window, with the night coming, and the crescent moon falling behind the trees.

Miles asked to be allowed to tell of their engagement to some of his friends, but Helen would not consent. "Not until you have taken your degree, anyway," she said.

If Boler could have seen him there his suspicions that Helen and Miles were engaged would have been fully confirmed. But Boler didn't see them there; no one saw them; and they cooed away until a sound from the chamber where Mrs. Longwood had rested — uninterrupted — brought Miles to his feet.

But oh, that unfortunate cut!

It was quite late in the evening. They had all been to the various halls where dancing was going on, had lingered in the yard, strolling up and down under the old Elms hung with myriads of colored lanterns, listening to the college songs of the Glee Club, and had now come back for one or two final waltzes out under the huge white tent among the palms and colored lights back of Beck Hall.

Boler was still faithful to his charge, and was doing his best to give Mrs. Longwood a good time. Miles had no occasion to try to do the same for Helen. They had been together quite constantly, and when they entered Beck and went down the flight of canvassed steps which led out on the lawn, they began to feel quite at home again.

There was a waltz going on. The two caught it up with life and joined the dancers.

It was a happy dance, and when the music ceased they were warm and breathless. Miles suggested a quiet stroll. They walked about under the palms, and finally came to a bower that seemed made for shy lovers. It was shaded from the light and was dark and cool.

They sat down. What they said was what all lovers say; what they did, bold lovers do,— but that terrible cut,— and when the strains of the last waltz of the night came to them, they went out into the bright light, under the tent.

But oh, that terrible cut! What mischief had it done?

There across the white cheek of Helen Rove was the counterpart of the cut Alfred Miles had given himself that morning.

The dancing had evidently started the blood; and in his love he had —

But what should he do? He stood as if turned to stone. There they were under the bright light, with a throng of people about them. A little knot of men, his intimate friends, were already shouting themselves hoarse at the open joke, and giving cheers for "Miles," while Helen, poor girl, all unaware of her terrible predicament, blushed until the tell-tale streak of crimson his cheek had left upon hers faded away in her own glowing color.

They got away somehow. And when, a little later, Miles asked Helen if she had any objections to his telling of their engagement to a few of his friends, she answered him, half tearfully, half smilingly:

"Oh, no, Allie. We can't do anything else now; let's publish it."

They had many presents when they were married, but the one over which they seemed to enjoy themselves the most, and laughed until they both cried, was one which came from the faithful Boler. It was in a crimson plush case; and before opening the case they tried to guess what it was.

Helen guessed a breast-pin.

Miles guessed a pipe.

They were both wrong.

It was a beautiful pearl-handled razor, upon the blade of which was engraved:

A. J. M. – H. S. R.,
HARVARD CLASS DAY, 1889.

Case Bull, '92.

GOODALE came to college what might be called a religious tough. One evening, when he and Horton and a few friends were discussing a certain divinity student, Goodale remarked : "All ministers are hypocrites." It was a very indiscreet remark to make in a general company. Among the men who heard him were one or two sincere Christians, and a number of others who held religion sacred,— sacred from everyday use or outside criticism. Consequently, Goodale was severely rebuked in the incoherent and violent discussion which his remark provoked. He was silenced, more from the volume and loudness of his opponents' arguments than from their force.

Goodale was rather proud of his agnosticism, although he said, and sincerely thought, that he would give almost anything to have the serene faith of some people. To Horton this impiousness of Goodale's was especially unpleasant. He was himself rather devout, and Goodale's agnosticism seemed to him cheap, and unworthy of a man with high ideals. He tried to convert him by argument, and by taking him to chapel.

Goodale had a sincere admiration and liking for Horton, and felt flattered at the value Horton set on his soul. He went willingly to chapel with him,— unless he had some studying to do, or some girl he wanted to call on,— enjoyed the music and criticised the minister.

"The trouble with you," said Horton to him, one Sunday night in his Junior year, "is that you don't go to church in the right spirit."

"You are mistaken," answered Goodale earnestly. "I went tonight with the wish to be improved, and not to find fault. I tried to fix my mind on the services and forget all else. I looked at the minister: he was a coarse-looking man, with fat, puffy cheeks. He stood up in the pulpit to give out the hymn. He opened his mouth to speak; it looked wide and black, in consonance with the rest of his face.

"'Let us sing the two hundred and thirty-fourth hymn,' he said solemnly; 'the two hun–dred and thir–ty-fourth.'"

"It's a nice way to condemn a man for his looks and the way he gives out his hymns," interrupted Horton.

"And then he preached about a harp and a lamb, somehow, and I couldn't make head or tail out of it; though I ought to, for his words came slowly and distinctly, with ev–er–y syl–la–ble sep–ar–ate–ly pronounced, like the words in 'Life's Primer,' only not half so bright. 'It is hard not to lin–ger on the beau–ti–ful image that is gi–ven to us,'—and evidently it was too hard for him, for he had lingered and lingered till I thought I should die."

Horton sat in silence, while Goodale continued vehemently:

"Although I tried my best to follow, I couldn't help thinking how much his style would be benefited by English 12, and how much English C would help his argumentative powers. Argument! He could no more argue than he could fly straight to heaven. He made assertions: 'There is no good outside of Christianity'; 'If religion is morality tinged with emotion, it is a base thing.' Then, since no one contradicted him, he made other assertions: 'A minority in this world can be good without religion,' and then he prayed for 'The emotion which is religion.'"

Goodale stopped and poked the fire with an energy such as Luther might have shown when he threw the ink-bottle at the Devil. Then he continued more quietly:

"When we read a novel, we probably read what has taken six months to write; when we go to a concert, we hear music that may have taken a year to compose: but when we go to church, we hear something on the most difficult subject in the universe, on which a second-rate man has probably spent two days. When he prays, we hear a string of incoherent, drivelling pieces of advice to God, interspersed with protestations of our own inferiority and humility, and ending up with the hope that, nevertheless, God will act on our suggestions."

This little ebullition took place during the fall of Goodale's Junior year. A few months later, just before Christmas, the renowned Dr. Burton from Liverpool paid Harvard a short visit. Goodale happened to hear him preach, the first Sunday that he was here, and while listening to him he forgot all about the minister's looks and Harvard's English courses. He heard a man speaking: a man who had temptations as other men had, and who did not seem

to have put off his earthly robe of human passions
and put on a saintly robe of Christian perfectness
as easily as one changes a foot-ball suit for one of
broadcloth.   Dr. Burton seemed to address himself
directly to Goodale as one man to another.   He
did not prate about harps and lambs and girding
up of loins; he did not hurl fiery denunciations at
the Pharisees, nor blame other peoples and other
times: but he spoke directly to Goodale of his
own commonplace temptations and unpicturesque
sorrows; and he spoke sympathetically, and under-
standingly, not with the unhumanness of a con-
descending god.

Goodale went to hear Dr. Burton every chance
he got during the next few weeks.   On the evening
before the Christmas recess, Dr. Burton was to give
the students an informal talk in Holden Chapel.
When Goodale got to the door he found the room
so full that he could not enter.   He therefore went
round to a side window that was open, and stood
there with some other students listening to Dr.
Burton's words.   That evening Dr. Burton spoke
in even a more personal tone than before; and
there was not a note that rang false through it
all.   He spoke of study and athletics; and it was
evident that the athletics were not merely put in
for oratorical purposes,— Doctor Burton spoke like a
man who knew the difference between putting the
shot and pole-vaulting.

When at last the Doctor began to pray, Goodale
took off his cap and bowed his head.   Next to him
was standing a handsome, dissipated-looking student.   After a moment's hesitation, he, too, took off

his hat. When the prayer was done, the students at the window went away in different directions, each one avoiding the other's eyes.

Goodale walked slowly homeward, more moved towards religion than he had ever been before in his life. He tried to think of some sacrifice that he might make in order to prove his earnestness to himself. When he got to his room he wrote half a dozen letters to Doctor Burton to thank him for what he had done for him; but none of them suited him, and he threw them all into the grate. Then he put out his lamp and sat for a long time watching the lumps of cannel coal that he put on the fire split up and burn brightly for a while, and then relapse into the normal flameless glow of the fire. He was still hunting for the great leaf that he was to turn over. When at last he found it, he groaned.

"I can't do it: make up to that vile Slynie,— I haven't spoken to the beggar since I came to college."

It wasn't very pleasant, the idea of apologizing to a fellow whom you despised, and whom you had insulted, and treated as almost below contempt. It wasn't romantic a bit, this becoming a Christian, if one had to shake hands — Ugh! the bare idea made his right hand feel greasy. But Goodale made up his mind to it at last, and went to bed with a conscience easier for the pleasant Christmas vacation that he was going home the next day to enjoy.

Towards the end of his Senior year, Goodale was sitting with Horton on the steps of Matthews, when a little man passed with the pleasant smile of a popular man. He was to be a minister, but he didn't speak of it any oftener than was necessary. He was very popular with most fellows.

"It makes me awfully tired to hear that man tell smutty stories," said Horton. "I don't pretend to be a saint myself, but I think a theologue should be a little better than the common run. It isn't as if it were a great temptation. One might forgive a minister for drinking or even for committing adultery. But this petty viciousness is disgusting."

"Half the ministers are damned hypocrites anyway," growled Goodale. Which showed that Goodale had modified his original assertion by half. He had never shaken hands with Slynie.

Kenneth Brown.

ANOTHER MAN'S MOTHER.

THE sultry May afternoon was turning into night, and Harvard, having had dinner, was taking it easy for an hour or so. After the burden and heat of the day, with its lectures and grinding and ball-games, everybody was in a mood for this relaxation, and the yard was dotted with little groups of students, whose garments of many colors appeared more picturesque than ever in the soft twilight. On the steps of one of the dormitories, a detachment of the Glee Club was singing sentimental ditties, encouraged at every pause by cries for " mo–o–re," which came through the darkness, long drawn out and plaintive, like the howling conventionally attributed to lost spirits.

A jumble of many sounds floated up through the branches of the elms and into 99 Weldworthy, where Mr. G. T. Tarleton was lying on a divan, and wishing that the singing might go on forever. When it stopped, he supposed that he should have to get up and go to grinding Fine Arts, and he was in no temper for Fine Arts then. Being for some reason or other in the incipient stages of the blues, he was moody and restless, and wanted somebody to talk to. That afternoon he had played tennis with a girl of his acquaintance, and had also met most of his college friends, notwithstanding which he felt now as though he were an outcast from his kind. It occurred to him that it might be a good idea to go and see a certain fellow in the next hall, and leave grinding until afterwards.

Outside, the Glee Club stopped singing, and Tarleton was getting ready to rise, when there came a light knock at his door and he rolled lazily off the lounge and went to open it. A woman carrying a heavy satchel stood there, and Tarleton could see by the uncertain light that though she looked fatigued, her face had a glad and eager expression.

"Joe?" she said, questioningly, and then seeing her mistake, she shrank back.

"I—I beg your pardon. I thought that Joe—that Mr. Tarleton roomed here," she said, with a gasp which was half a sob. She was tired out with a hard day's journey, and the disappointment was great.

"My name is Tarleton," replied the young man, quickly, "but not Joe. Probably you have mistaken the address. But come in, please, and I will try to find the one you want."

He took her satchel, and she followed him hesitatingly into the room, and sat down in the chair which he offered her. Tarleton lit the gas, and the woman looked about her with a slightly bewildered expression. She had never been in a room of this kind before, and the medley of shingles, boxing-gloves, and photographs, with some books in the background, evidently puzzled her.

"You wished to find Mr. Joe Tarleton?" he asked.

"Yes," she replied, simply; "he is my boy. I could not remember his address for sure, and a man that I asked told me that he roomed here."

"Must have got the addresses mixed," said
Tarleton. "Let me look it up in the Catalogue."

He took down the red-covered book, and while
he was turning its pages, he had a chance to study
the face of his visitor. Insensibly, he began to forget his former ill-humor while doing so, it was such
a sweet and attractive face, with its expression of
mingled courage and simplicity. The hair about
the temples was already gray, and care had made
some wrinkles on the forehead, but the mouth was
still as pleasant and the steady gray eyes as clear
as when they had belonged to a girl of twenty,—
though that must have been more than twenty years
ago. Evidently this was not a rich woman, for her
dress was very plain, and the crape on her bonnet
a little worn in places. Tarleton, as he watched
her, wondered what errand had brought her up to
Cambridge, and what manner of person the Joe that
she was seeking might be.

"A grind very likely," he said to himself; "or
perhaps it's some young fool who tries to be fast
and lets his mother work for him. I've known of
that kind. She looks as if she had worried."

"Is that it?" he said aloud. "J. C. Tarleton,
29 Holworthy street."

"Oh, yes," she replied; "that is the name and
the address, too; I remember now. Forgive me
for having been so stupid. You see," she added,
apologetically, "I am not used to going around
strange places at night, and I think that I got a
little confused. I tried to get into that white building over there first."

She smiled, and he, watching her, smiled also,

and felt at the same moment that they were on very good terms somehow.

"And so your name is Tarleton, too?" she asked with interest.

"Yes," he replied; "George Tarleton, Junior Class."

"Why, Joe is a Junior, too," she said; "you must know him, of course, if you are both in the same class."

"I — er — I believe that I do know him slightly," replied G. T. Tarleton. He vaguely remembered now that there was a grind of the same name in his class, and that he had once spoken to him in the Freshman year.

"I supposed that the men in the same class knew each other well," she said.

"Well, there are a good many of us," he replied, "and we go in for different things, of course. Your son, I believe, is a — he studies, I mean."

"I thought," said she, "that you all did that."

"Some of us do everything but that," he replied, with a laugh; but the words sounded a little cheap as he spoke them, and he colored under her clear gaze. It occurred to him how funny the situation was, how absurd that they should be talking thus confidentially; and yet he rather enjoyed it.

"I don't just see," she said, "why young men should care to stay here unless it is to study."

"I mean," said he, hastily, "that your son is a very much better student than I am. He is sure of graduating with honors, isn't he?"

"He is very anxious to; but I don't know whether he can. He has not been very well, and he seems discouraged these days. So I came here to try and cheer him up a little."

"Do you mean," asked G. T. Tarleton, "that his health won't allow him to finish?"

"It is not that," she replied, and then she stopped, embarrassed. "I am afraid that he won't be able to afford another year. I have tried to help him along, and Joe has done what work he could at tutoring, but somehow he says that he does not make much of a success of it. It must take a great deal to live here?"

"Yes," said George, vaguely; "it is rather an expensive place."

"Joe says," she continued, "that he can't get through a year here less than $500, and I don't think that he is extravagant. Most young men spend as much as that, I suppose."

"Ye–s–s," replied George; "I should say so. Some spend more."

"Yes," she continued; "Joe has written to me about that. He says that some of the students here, who have a great deal of money, spend all their time amusing themselves, and never study any, that he can see." Here she stopped and seemed to remember that the person before her had just acknowledged as much. "But I am sure," she continued, hurriedly, "that you wouldn't do like that."

"Why do you think so?" asked Tarleton.

"I am sure you wouldn't," she said, warmly, and then checking herself, she rose to go. "I don't know why I have been running on like this," she added; "I hope I have not troubled you. It has

been very kind of you, sir, to let me rest here."
And she looked gratefully at the big young man
who had offered her his hospitality.

"Mrs. Tarleton," said George,— and it seemed
strange to address her in that way — "won't you
let me take you to 29 Holworthy street. I know
where it is, and it will not be the least trouble to
me."

They went down and walked along together, talking as confidentially as though they had known one
another for twenty years instead of for about as
many minutes. They found the street and the house
where Joe lodged, and G. T. Tarleton waited for a
moment while Mrs. Tarleton went up the steps.
Before she could ring, the door opened, and a lank
young fellow, with baggy trousers and the external
attributes of a chronic grind, came forth.

"Why, mother."

"Joe, my boy."

G. T. Tarleton walked away into outer darkness.

Two or three mornings after this, Joe Tarleton
went to attend a lecture in Philosophy 27, feeling
more hopeful than usual. His mother had started
for home that morning, after a short visit with her
son which had put a new heart into him. G. T.
Tarleton also took the course, and Joe kept watching him with interest, for his mother had told about
her little adventure. And so when, after the lecture,
G. T. Tarleton came toward him and seemed inclined to say something, Joe remarked awkwardly:

"I want to thank you, Mr. Tarleton, for your
kindness to my mother the other night. She told
me about it, and wanted me to thank you."

"Very happy to have been of service," said the other, and then he added in a business-like tone:

"I say, Mr. Tarleton, you take this course,— do you ever tutor in it?"

"Why," replied Joe, hesitatingly, "I should like to, but I am not a very good tutor. Really, you could find some much better men in the course."

"What have you got in it so far?"

"B+. Several men have done better."

"That's all right," said G. T. Tarleton, briskly; "anybody who can get B+ can teach me a great deal about the stuff. And if you are willing to tutor me, I'll come around tomorrow evening."

He did go around, and easily secured Joe's services, although he insisted on paying more than the latter asked. The finals being close at hand, they went to work immediately, and got along together very well. They were about as dissimilar as any two young men well could be, and the slow, deliberate grind used to stop work sometimes, and stare wonderingly at his pupil who represented such a different kind of life from his own. He himself, being poor and proud, was inclined to be a little stiff toward the other man, and it amazed him that the latter seemed so determined to make advances. The most astonishing thing of all was the unaccountable interest which G. T. Tarleton took in Joe's mother. One night Joe happened to mention her, and said that she was coming to see him in a few days.

"Is she," asked G. T. Tarleton, with enthusiasm. "I hope that I can see her, too. You know I met her once; and I should like to again."

"Well, I don't wonder," said Joe, slowly. "I don't know what I should do without her. I don't believe that I should be going through college."

"You're a lucky fellow," growled the swell, "to have such a mother."

"Why," asked Joe, sympathetically, "haven't you got one?"

"Oh, yes," answered G. T. Tarleton, shortly; "I've got one."

A picture of his mother occupied the place of honor in his room, and represented her as a handsome, languid woman with the same rather haughty cast of features that her son had. She spent most of her time in Europe, and George could not remember when she had ever shown any particular interest in him. The helpful sympathy and comfort which Joe Tarleton received, had all the charm of novelty to the other man.

Thanks to Joe's tutoring, G. T. Tarleton was enabled to pass the examination in Philosophy 27 triumphantly with a C—; and in return he enabled the grind to pay his term bills, and to stay the year out. Nor did the mutual services of the two end with this. The next year, G. T. Tarleton employed Joe constantly as his tutor, and, moreover, sent some of his friends to him,—whereby more than one sporting career in college was prolonged. Twice during this time Mrs. Tarleton came up to Cambridge to visit her son, and on each occasion George managed to see her and to have a little confidential talk with her. He told her about his life at Harvard, grown better of late because of her, and praised up Joe; and she told him that she felt almost as though she had two boys in college.

He had her at his spread on Class Day, and surprised people by the attention which he paid to her. Later, in the evening, when the yard, with its lights and music, was like a piece out of fairy-land, he took pains to guide her around, for the simple country woman was a little bewildered in the midst of such a crowd. They stopped at last in a quiet place to listen to the Glee Club sing, and to talk a little to one another.

" I hope that you have had a pleasant time," said G. T. Tarleton.

" Yes, I have," she answered. " You have made it very nice for me, I am sure. How kind you have been to Joe and to me both."

" Oh, don't mention it, please," said he.

" I hope that I shall hear from you sometimes," she said. " I shall be very glad always to know how you are getting along — just as much as if you were my own son."

" I am awfully glad to hear you say so," replied G. T. Tarleton, looking very much pleased, and speaking with boyish bluntness. Somehow he never could say bright things to her.

" I feel sometimes," she continued, " as though I didn't have any right to be so much interested in you, but I can't help it. In some ways I think almost more about you than I do about Joe even. You see, Joe is made for books, and he doesn't care much about other things, but you are different. I can't just say what I mean, but it seems to me as if you had more chances to be either good or bad.

than Joe has. And I do hope that you will do well."

"I certainly shall try to," replied G. T. Tarleton. And he felt just then that, sooner than disappoint her, he would try very hard.

At Commencement, Joe was happy because he had a *magna cum*, and G. T. Tarleton was equally so because he had a degree — a poor thing, as he expressed it, but his own. Toward the end of the day, the two classmates met, and stepped aside to shake hands, and to wish one another good luck. Joe seemed to have something on his mind, and was as awkward as only a young man can be when he has something to say which borders on the sentimental.

"I don't know how to thank you," said he. "I have been thinking it over, and I see that I could probably never have gone through here if it had not been for your help. I don't know why you have done it, but thank you."

"Oh, that's all right," said G. T. Tarleton almost as embarrassed as himself. "I am very glad if I have helped you any, but, to tell the truth, I didn't exactly do it on your account. You — er — you know your mother?"

"Why, yes," replied Joe, puzzled; "of course."

"Well," said G. T. Tarleton, flushing red, "I did it for her sake. And I say, old man, I wish that you would tell her so some time."

Mortimer Wilcox.

A FALLEN IDOL.

A T this juncture little Bill got out of his easy-chair and filled our mugs all around. Four mouths were simultaneously opened, four mugs were raised aloft, and four men kept the dead silence of him who is drinking beer. Then somebody suggested that the smooth-tongued Fred give us a tale, and we all composed ourselves to listen. Fred began:

"Did I ever tell you about Jim Hinkley? No? Well, he was a queer chap."

Here Fred paused and buried his face in the beer-mug. We all waited patiently till Fred went on:

"He was a large, powerful fellow, with a gruff voice, a surly air, and a cynical way of talking about religion and goodness. He said nobody in the world was really good, that he himself was as bad as the lot of 'em, and he used to regale us with stories of some of the tricks he had played on teachers before he came to college, and of lots of mean things that he professed to have done, by way of proving his point: that it was a wicked world. We used to believe in him, and considered him one of the wickedest men around, who would some day become a regular man-hater, like the magicians of old. When he came to college, his depraved propensities" (Fred was fond of long words) "took a broader range. He studied philosophy, and loved to gather six or eight of us in his room, and disprove the truth of the Scriptures, trying to instill in our minds a callous, materialistic way of looking at things. He was very fond of the doctrine of the survival of the fittest, and strongly believed in its application to human affairs. Finally, we came to worship him as a hero of hard-heartened cynicism, as a prince of evil-wishing, just as the fallen spirits must look up to Beelzebub.

"But I was sometimes suspicious of our chief, for an incident of his school-days came to my mind.

"It was the winter before we all passed our finals and the weather was horribly cold. I was walking down Boylston street towards Washington one raw Monday afternoon. As I passed the entrance of a narrow alley, I happened to look in. There was a large boy or man standing with his back to me, looking down into the face of a shivering girl, as dirty as she was poor. She was looking up into the man's face with a queer expression of wonder and gratitude. He seemed to be talking kindly to her, and presently I saw him slip something bright into her frozen little hand, at which her lips seemed to move in thanks. I was getting interested when the man turned as if to go — then I saw who it was and hurried away, half disappointed and half pitying. That very morning he had confided to me some devilish design of his to wreck our teacher's peace of mind.

"The remembrance of this incident used to haunt me like Banquo's ghost and I began to wish I had not seen it. But as years went on, and Jim grew more thoroughly set in his cynical philosophy, I began to consider the thing as a good joke that he had played on himself, and nothing more."

Here Fred got up, filled his pipe and began pacing the room, dolefully blowing out huge clouds of smoke.

"Let's hear the rest," I urged. Fred shook his head gloomily.

"What! is it so bad as all that?" asked somebody, sympathetically.

"Yes, it's pretty bad," said Fred; "you don't know what stock I once set on Jim's strength of character."

But we finally induced Fred to finish. He went on:

"It happened in the middle of his Sophomore year. One morning, Jim was waked up by a terrible noise in the next room. Going to the door of the study, he saw the porter firing pieces of coal at the blower, which resounded loudly at each stroke. He seemed to be full as a goat. Jim told him to stop; then the porter turned the battery on Jim. Jim was too good a man to stand being pelted with coals by a Weld Hall porter, so he went for him. The noise they made together brought in the proctor, who declared that Jim had been drinking, and told him he should be reported to the Dean.

"That afternoon two people went up to the Dean: the first was the porter, who liked Jim too much to get him into trouble. The porter confessed that it was all his fault. The Dean gave him one of his sweetly dubious smiles, and said the porter must go. The porter went. Later, Jim appeared. By this time, the Dean had assumed a very stern look. He told Jim that a great disturbance was reported as having taken place in his room that morning, and that the proctor said that he, Mr. Hinkley, had been drinking, had not come home till daylight, had found the porter peacefully making the fire, had kicked him because he was in his way, then had hit the porter with his fist, and had ended by causing great disorder in a college building.

"During all this talk Jim had been smiling softly to himself, though he appeared somewhat astonished. The Dean closed by saying: 'And now, Mr. Hinkley, I must know whose fault it was; this report may be incorrect. Only you and the porter know who began it. If the porter, he shall be discharged; if you, you must be suspended. Tell me on your word of honor whose fault it was.'

"The Dean looked searchingly at Jim and Jim looked searchingly at the Dean. Then Jim said: 'It was my fault.'

"The Dean seemed satisfied, and Jim was turning away with an exultant look in his eyes and his old cynical smile playing around his lips, when suddenly the Dean jumped up, seized Jim by the hand and gave him a hearty shake. All he said was: 'Mr. Hinkley, I shall not discharge the porter — for your sake,' and again the Dean smiled.

"Jim shot a quick glance at that smile, took in the situation at once and made a hasty exit, looking like a dog that has been beaten."

"Or a bad man found out in a good deed," chimed in little Bill.

"Good nothing," retorted Fred. "I tell you it was awful."

And then little Bill got up and gave us all some more beer.

Eugene Warner.

"*MESSIEURS, faites vos jeus!*" the croupier's tired, nasal tones rang from one green table to another in that grand *Salle de Jeu* in the Casino — that is, the *Cercle* at the bustling little Savoy spa, Aix-les-bains.

Any cynic walking through that vast hall and looking at the wealth of the ponderous chandeliers, the thickness and richness of the hangings, and the lavish dollar-an-inch look of the splendid wall-paper, would smile scornfully at the aspirants to rapid wealth clustered nervously and patiently around the four great gaming tables. For where did the money come from that gave such an air of luxury to the place? The white face of that man wandering blindly out of the hall would have told at once.

Of all there who believed most sincerely in luck at baccarat, one was now sitting perched on a high chair, just back of the circle of the ten men who, divided into fives by the croupier and banker, leaned over the green fish-pond. She was short and well-dressed and pretty — and so, American.

Of all there who smiled the most cynically, sauntering through that pampered palace, was one who was tall and military in moustache and shoulders, both of which had an energetic set of curves and angles. He was dressed in tight, fawn-colored trousers, slate-colored cutaway, and queer-looking patent leathers — so he was French.

The little woman on the high chair was slight, blue-eyed and irregularly lovely. The man who sauntered cynically was dark and decidedly hand-some.

Once, as she looked up to reckon her gains mentally, and once when he looked down to see who had just bought the bank for such a ruinous pile of francs, their eyes met. Being a Frenchman, he grew interested, and wanted just such another accidental glance. So he found a place across the table, and, under pretence of following the game, watched her.

She had bad luck from that minute. Each time as the croupier called the banker's cards, and each time as the cards at her end of the table turned up unfavorable as compared to the banker's, she made a little grimace of petulance. The man with the military moustache saw that grimace, and immediately liked it. He hoped she would lose again. She did. The grimace reappeared. The man of the military shoulders determined to meet the owner of the grimace; and wished her a continuance of bad luck. She had more bad luck, and after losing fourteen successive times, and making fourteen petulant grimaces, she left. The cynic returned to his sauntering.

Baccarat is played from noon till midnight — ladies usually gamble in the middle of the afternoon. The next afternoon, the little American woman was again on her high chair, as hopeful as ever. At the same time the big Frenchman sauntered in, as cynical as ever. He stood opposite her and wished her ill luck. She had very ill luck, and was lavish with the most delicious grimaces the big Frenchman had ever seen.

This expression — *la moue*, as they call it over there, — was quite new to him. When a French-woman feels annoyed, she draws up the corners of her shoulders and draws down the corners of her mouth. But this American left her shoulders alone. She just protruded her little upper lip, at the same time drawing her chin into a combination of delight-ful wrinkles, and contracting her brows over her very blue eyes and very dark lashes. It was the gentle remonstrance against fate of a spoilt but still sweet-natured child.

The Frenchman was at the *Cercle* every day for a week, and saw and fell in love with that *moue*. He proved so efficacious a Hoodoo that after a week the little American stopped gambling. She went to the afternoon concerts instead, and sat be-side her big, wealthy-looking American papa, and did needle-work.

The grimace had vanished. But the cynic with the military shoulders and slate-colored cutaway was ingenious. He bribed small boys to pester her with things to buy, like candy, withered cycla-men and Italian toys. Then he stood off in the vista of columns and watched her as the little nuisances importuned her, and so he caught that divine grimace again.

Finally he compassed an introduction, and when her father learned that he was a lieutenant in the French army and the eldest son of a count, and when he had devoted himself to the fair pouter for a month, they became engaged. Then after a while they were married in the gilt drawing-room of the Continental, and lived in Paris.

Then he learned that she was from Chicago, without knowing what it all meant. But they were awfully happy.

It was the grimace and its little romance that spoiled their lives. He made too good a husband for the little American woman. She had no occasion to pout when he was around. He began to miss the grimace so much that he could not live without seeing it, so he practised spilling coffee at breakfast and claret at dinner. Finally she saw through his little game, and refused to make the desired *moue*.

Then they came to an understanding: he could not live with her unless she pouted; she would not live with him if he kept doing things to annoy her. So they agreed to separate.

That was five years ago. Now, she is living in Chicago with her father, and is going to send her son to West Point, to get him a pair of military shoulders and (if possible) a military moustache. She lives in the hope of seeing them reproduced on a creature who will not try to make her angry for his own joy.

He is spending his summers at Aix, sauntering through the *Salle de Jeu*, smiling more cynically than ever, and trying to call up memories.

Eugene Warner.

IT was noon on the first of February, and his swear-off was ended. He unlocked the drawer in his centre table where all his pipes had lain for a month: and he gazed at them lovingly as he took them out one by one.

There was the briarwood bull-dog which he had used on last summer's cruise. He had bought it at Falmouth in a small shop. It was cheap and had a rubber mouth-piece; but the bowl was colored a rich brown, and it was crusted inside, and smoked mild and sweet. Therefore he took it up tenderly and laid it on his smoking table.

Then came the clay, looking like an old-fashioned powder-horn without the cover. It was black as jet near the mouth-piece and shaded off to light grey round the edge of the bowl. How rank and strong it was, and how his sister hated it. He only smoked it to plague her, for it made him nervous for hours afterward.

Next he saw the swell English briar which his father had given him, and which he never used, for it was clumsy and dragged on his teeth; and there was a long student pipe that he bought three years ago in Heidelberg; and a delicate little wexel-wood, a philopena from her.

He took all these out and laid them side by side on the smoking table,— all but the wexel, which he put in his waistcoat pocket; it was so very light and slender.

He filled the old briar, lighted it and puffed away as he looked at the remaining pipes in the drawer. There was the pipe which he had won at the raffle, unsmoked as yet. It was meerschaum, ghostly pale; and on it lay a sleeping woman with charms unconcealed. He remembered his Aunt Matilda's face when she came to visit him one day and saw the pipe lying on his table. He laughed at that memory, and took the pipe and placed it high above the others on a tobacco box.

Then came cigarette and cigar holders too numerous to mention, mostly Christmas and birthday presents. He never used them, but still they filled up space. So he scattered them carelessly among the pipes; but at last he saw his treasure. He took out of the drawer an enormous sealskin case and opened it carefully. Inside was a meerschaum, a head of Mephistopheles colored to perfection,— everywhere a deep, rich brown; and its long, pointed nose, its small, slanting eyes, its thin, sneering lips, its slender moustache and goatee, made it look very diabolical. It was this pipe that had made him quit smoking. He held it carefully by the stem, and the firelight flickered on its keen features and it seemed to wink at him.

There was a strange legend connected with this pipe — how it was made by enchantment in the midst of the Hartz Mountains, and how one who once smoked it could never leave off smoking again. A simple peasant in Germany had told him this tale, and had probably got an extra price for the story. "Well, old boy," he said with a sigh, "you've got the better of me again, and I guess you always will."

H. H. Chamberlin, Jr., '95.

MARY KELLY'S LAPDOG.

CASTLE Island is a starving little village in the heart of County Kerry. The people there are as simple and as kind-hearted as any in Ireland, but a dozen years ago they thought nothing of shooting a landlord or an agent now and then. All that is changed today; the blue-coated constabulary overrun the place; the people are cowered and spiritless; and it is only on a fair or market day that they dare indulge their heredi-tary fondness for fighting and ructions.

I happened to be in Castle Island on fair day. I was wakened early in the morning by the pro-longed squealing of a family of heartbroken pigs offered for sale in a wagon directly below my window. For all strange sights, commend me to the five hundred Irish people who, massed among carts and animals of all descriptions, jabber and gesticulate, drink and grow pathetic, and fight and break heads, all for the ostensible purpose of buy-ing and selling some spavined horses and lean-looking pigs.

I did daring deeds that day, to the astonishment of the hotel waiter who acted as my guide. He admired my originality and independence, but it cut him to the heart to think that I should see but an indifferent fair.

"Myself can remember when an Irish fair was worth the whistle," he said in a half soliloquy. "In thim days, the police was a lot of weeshy little gossoons that daren't lay a finger on a man if he

was drunk, and if one o' thim showed himself at a
fight, he got a polthogue on the gob that would
dazzle the eyes out of a blindman's head! It
would warm the heart o' ye to have seen a fight in
thim days, with the crashing and shouting, and
slipping and smashing,— men dropping by the
dozens, and the women screeching like mad, and
the kippeens — the sticks, ye know,— blackening
the air! Oh, then, but it was beautiful entirely!"

He was interrupted by a shout from the upper
end of the street. An old, dishevelled woman, with
a basket on her arm, was swaggering majestically
through a crowd of jeering men. At her heels
followed a yellow cur — a queer little mongrel, with
a stub of a tail, and a rakish, battered air that was
altogether Irish.

" 'Tis the foine body-guard ye have there, Mary,"
said one of the crowd, pointing to the cur.

"Sure, every lady must have her lapdog," said
the old woman, gathering her shawl about her with
an affectation of elegance that made the crowd roar
with delight.

"Who is this?" I asked my guide.

"Old Mary Kelly, sir, that lives on the road to
Kilcrea. She buys clams from a fisherman at
Bantry, and sells 'em on fair day, and every penny
she airns goes for the dhrink. She's the divil himself when the dhrop's in her."

It was very evident that this was one of the
occasions when the "dhrop was in her." She was
very drunk indeed. She reeled over to the curb,
and was just about to fall headlong, when she man-

aged to recover herself and sit down composedly. The crowd huddled itself about her expectantly.

"Oh, wurrah! but I'm in the height of affliction, heartbroken entirely,— a poor, lone woman, wid niver a friend in the world, barring Cornalius — me dog, Cornalius."

The dog acknowledged this remark by affectionately rubbing his mangy back against her knee.

"He's a livin' reminder av his masther — my poor, dead Mike, that was shot down by the polis at Kilcrea. When Mike was lyin' on his death-bed, wid the rattle in his throat and the mist in his eye, he called me to him. 'Mary,' says he, in a voice as wake as wather, 'Mary,' says he, 'be good to the dog, poor crathur, Cornalius Agrippa.'"

"Cornalius Agrippa, do you call the dog?" said one of the crowd. "Sure, that's a brave name for such a rag of a baste."

"It's a Bible name, I'm thinkin', Mary," said an old, wizened man, with an air of importance.

"Thrue for you, Misther Lanigan," answered Mary proudly; "'twas Father Mahoney that christened the dog. He followed me into Mass one morning — the crathur — and divil resave the lie if he didn't try to cross himself with the paw of him."

"I mind the day well, Mary," shouted the old man.

"Hould yer whisht, Lanigan!" growled the crowd. "Can't ye let Mary tell the story herself?"

Lanigan fell back abashed, and Mary continued with an air of increased importance:

"'Oh, the sanctity of the animal!' says the Father to me; 'oh, the piety of the baste! Sure, a dog like that is a model of a Christian. We'll be sendin' him out as a missionary to the haythens in foreign parts. Oh, Mary,' says he, 'don't that bring the blush to yer face, don't that shrivel up the soul of ye wid shame? Here's a dog that knows his jooty betther than a Christian.'"

Mary paused for a moment to recover her wind, while the crowd threw admiring glances at the dog, who was biting savagely at a flea.

"'And what do you call the baste, Mary,' says the Father to me. 'It's Mike's dog he was,' says I, 'and Mike called him Red Pepper.' 'Oh, then he's a highly-seasoned baste,' says the Father, 'but sure a dog like that desarves a more dignified appellation. We must give him a Bible name, Mary,' says the Priest. 'Call him Cornalius — Cornalius Agrippa.'"

There was a stir in the crowd. A constable in a uniform was elbowing his way through. Mary Kelly pushed back her hair and tried to steady herself. The dog was on his feet, growling like a small thunderstorm.

"Come now," said the police, "move on, the lot of ye! And you, old woman, take yerself out of this before I run you in!"

Mary glared at him, her arms akimbo, while she swayed back and forth. The police drew his club.

"Do you hear me, ould strap! 'Tis you I'm talkin' to. Your road is waitin' for you!"

"You'd betther be goin' while yer shoes is good, Mary," said old Lanigan, in a whisper of friendly warning.

"I will, if it's plazing to me, and not unless," was Mary's defiant answer.

The police waited for no more words, but let his club do the talking. The crowd broke away precipitately.

I had seized my guide by the arm. "How pale you are," he said, with a forced laugh. "Sure, that's nothing! Nothing at all, faith."

"It's enough for me," I said. "Come away!"

I turned to look back once more. The old woman was lying with her head on the curb, while Cornelius Agrippa licked the blood from her face.

Townsend Walsh, '95.

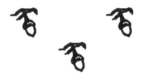

FOR UNKNOWN REASONS.

THE staid old Methodist village of Baden had suddenly become imbued with the gambling spirit. Shocking as was the fact, more shocking yet was it that the farmers, their wives, the pillars of the church, even the parson himself, were all interested in the result. The epidemic had originated in a most peculiar manner, and had confined itself to a single phase of disease. It had been neither base-ball, nor foot-ball, nor horse-racing, nor boat-racing, nor politics, which had been responsible, for in none of these things were the citizens of Baden remotely interested, and to none of these things had the rage for betting extended. The whole trouble had originated in the speculation as to the probable marriage of the belle of the town.

When the five McKee brothers — John, James, Jerome, Jay and Jacob — all took it into their heads to go calling on Isabelle Fulton, people regarded it as a remarkable freak of unanimity in one family, and pointed out the five brothers as models of fraternal affection and deference. But when the five continued to call, and, at last, palpably with amorous intent, things became positively serious. From five affectionate, unselfish, unindividual brothers they were transformed in the popular mind into five quiet, but none the less dangerous and aggressive, enemies. The life of Baden had heretofore been free from rivalry and contention, but now those two factors had entered, and gambling is always where contention is. It had begun by Farmer Jones remarking before a crowd at Strock's grocery that he would bet on John, and the words had not been out of his mouth when Farmer Smith, whose pasture adjoined Jones's, stated that he would bet on Jacob. Within five minutes, every man in the store had out a little book or a piece of paper, and was jotting down in most approved form bets of all sizes, from a peck of sweet potatoes to a five-dollar bill, on who would win the hand of Isabelle.

When a sizable rock gets a good solid impetus down a hill, such as was given to this rock by this group of estimable citizens, it is apt to spread itself. It is probable that within two days Isabelle Fulton was the only person who had not bets upon the result. Certain it is that Mr. Fulton offered his wife a trip to town, and her choice of the ready-made dresses in any store, if she could pick the winner, while she, in return, offered to give Mr. Fulton apple dumplings for dinner every day in the year if his man was the right one. And each of the five candidates backed himself heavily, and seemed to have no lack of confidence as to the result. Winning qualities in all of them were so equally balanced that it was really hard to make any choice. John was a widower of thirty-five and not so good-looking as the rest, but he had more money than all of them put together. The others were all better mannered and better educated than John, and age did not play such an important part in their make-ups, particularly with Jacob, who was only nineteen.

What made it all the harder to bet, with any reasonable expectation of winning, was that, as far as one could judge, Isabelle treated all her suitors exactly alike. When they came to call on her, they all came in a bunch, as they seemed to think that it would be dishonorable to try to steal a march on one another, and they were determined that the warfare should be open. There were two methods which Isabelle employed in entertaining them. If she had plenty of time, she would call them in severally, beginning with John and ending with Jacob, and to each one she would talk for exactly fifteen minutes, while the others sunned themselves outside on the whitewashed fence. If she did not have much time to spare, she would call them all in together and talk right around the circle, treating all exactly alike. People knew, because those interested in the case hired little boys to watch through the window, and thus a sort of running bulletin of the progress of things was kept up.

One day, when she was receiving her callers separately, one of the little boys who had been stationed at the window rushed down to Strock's store, panting.

" She's jus' kissed John," he cried, as soon as he could get his breath.

There was a dead silence. Then a man rose who had all his money on the other four, and tried to hedge. He offered twenty-five to one on John, but there were no takers. A second little boy rushed in.

" She's jus' kissed James," he cried.

The man who had been trying to hedge sat down. John and James were now pitted against each other at bullish rates, while the stock of all the others had fallen away below par. A third little boy darted in.

" She's jus' kissed Jerome," was his report.

Shortly afterwards came the fourth little boy with the news that she had just kissed Jay, and then the stock market became afflicted with a sudden fit of depression. In a little while the fifth little boy ran in, all out of breath and looking as if he had something new. A big farmer grabbed the boy.

"Tell me," he said almost piteously, " has she kissed Jacob ? "

" No," cried the urchin, " but she put her arm around him an' sort o' cuddled up to him an' looked kind o' pleased."

" Gentlemen," said the big farmer impressively, " I am going to lay all my money on Jacob."

About two weeks later, all bets were declared off. For Isabelle had married a young doctor from the city.

Arthur S. Pier, '95.

THE LAW BREAKER.

WE had all been to the theatre, and, after the inevitable *soirée* at the Adams House, were strolling down Washington street to take the car for Cambridge. It was a moonlight night, but the buildings rose so high on either hand that the street lay quite dark in their shadow. The place usually so noisy was deserted and silent, and our steps rattled startlingly upon the pavement.

We were passing a court which lay in deep shadow on our left, when one of my comrades said in a low tone, "Let's step into White's for a minute." The proposition met with some little objection at first, but it was quickly silenced and we turned into the darkness. For myself, I did not even know what "White's" was; in my childlike innocence I supposed it must be an oyster house. My companions led the way some distance down the court, and stopped in front of a seemingly deserted house. All was silent. The block was dark from end to end. Overhead, the pale moon swam in little fleecy specks of cloud, but none of its light penetrated the gloomy court. My friends looked cautiously up the street in both directions, then turned and mounted the steps. The door offered no resistance. We entered the inner darkness and came to a second door, which was quickly opened from the inside by a fat little man in shirtsleeves. The fellows addressed him familiarly and stumbled on upstairs. As I passed him he winked good-naturedly. "Over or under twenty-one, I suppose," he said.

I climbed the stairs and entered a brilliantly lighted room. It was comparatively quiet. At one end a crowd of men were gathered closely about a long table. No one spoke. All were watching intently something moving in their midst. A peculiar whirring noise was in the air, as of a marble running in a plate. Finally the sound grew more rapid and stopped with a click. "Twenty-one red," said a man's voice in a low tone. There was a slight stir at the table, a noise as of chips being dealt out upon a hard surface, then the whirring sound began again, and again the men gathered closely round.

For a moment I hardly knew what was being done. Then I realized where I was. Oh, the feeling that swept over me at that realization — a mingled feeling of shame and mortification, and, I must confess, of wicked pleasure at satisfied curiosity! At last I was actually in a "gambling hell." How unlike a hell it seemed — the pleasant-faced guardian at the door, and the gentlemanly bearing of the men on the other side of the room. My conscience smote me. Ought I to stay? "Of course not," was my first thought; my duty was to leave at once. Then the thought came, "Now I am here, the harm is done, I might as well get the benefit of my sin. Besides, looking at it from another point of view, I ought to understand the game for the sake of experience." The temptation was too great — I resolved to remain.

The other fellows had moved over to the table. I followed and worked my way into the crowd. The men were too intent upon the board to notice my intrusion. A hanging lamp cast its yellow light down upon the cluster of heads bending over a table curiously marked out in squares and numbers. A large wheel in the centre of the table ran rapidly round and round, while at its edge circled a small black marble. The hub of the wheel was full of notches, and at last the ball dropped into one of them. There was a flutter of excitement. The man at the wheel said, "Eleven black," and another man opposite him, who sat with piles of bills and variously colored chips before him, swept the counters from most of the squares, added a few here and there, and tossed a roll of bills to the man next to me. "Won that time, by Gad!" said my neighbor, nonchalantly stuffing the bills into his pocket; "played the eleven eight times running." I looked into his face. I shall never forget it — a bloodless, dark, hollow face, sneering and cynical. "Good God!" I thought, "shall I ever look like that!"

I looked across the table. Ned caught my eye. He smiled and held up five chips, pointing to a black square on the table. Again the wheel began to whir and the men to lay down their piles of counters. The spirit was contagious. I tossed the man a bill and received ten chips in return. Trembling with excitement, I watched the others. The man next me laid three chips on a red square. I did the same. The ball stopped. "Thirty-five red." The man by the wheel swept the losing chips off the table. Pointing to mine, he inquired sharply, "Are those yours?" "Yes," I answered, blushing hotly. He threw two down and mechanically I picked them up. Again the wheel whirled.

I now felt more at ease and deposited my seven chips in various parts of the board with something like confidence. The ball stopped, and a second time the man paid me my winnings, for I had won. Again I placed my bets and then looked round the table. To my astonishment, I saw many familiar faces — faces that I saw every day in the class-room or the yard. Faces of fellows whom I had always thought manly and honorable. Instinctively I felt a feeling of aversion toward them. But were they worse than I?

And now, fired with excitement, I played on. With the usual luck of the beginner, I continued to win. It began to be noticed. Others stopped playing to watch me. With a kind of gratification I noticed that the rest were playing as I did. Time flew. I lost and won and lost again. At last I had but a dollar left. Almost wishing to lose, and have it over with, I placed it on the " double zero " at the head of the board. The men were playing high. The table was loaded with bills and counters. Round and round whirled the ball. There was a hush as its running grew faster and faster, and when it stopped there was a dead silence. The man at the wheel cried out, " Double zero, the bank wins ! " A murmur of disappointment went round the table, and I realized that all had lost but myself. They shoved a pile of bills over toward me. I took them and squeezed out from the crowd.

I went over to the door and looked back. The same scene was before me that had met my eye on entering. The same eager crowd was there and the same whirring of the wheel resounded in my ears.

But was *I* the same? As I stood there, I had no feeling of satisfaction at having won. The excitement had left me and I felt sorry that I had played. What right had I to the money of those men? I went downstairs and out into the street.

All was dark and quiet as before. The air above was filled with the soft moonlight. I started on, still holding in my hand the roll of bills that constituted my winnings. Suddenly, I saw before me the figure of a policeman. My heart sank. I knew I was a gambler. I crossed the street and sneaked by on the other side.

The car was rushing over Harvard Bridge. The water of the river sparkled and shone in the bright moonlight, and the lights of Boston twinkled behind us. I stood wretchedly looking on it all, still holding the money in my hand. We neared the centre of the bridge. Down below, the river ran smoothly and silently. An impulse seized me, and, with all my might, I threw the roll of bills from me over the bridge.

Philip Richards, '96·

MR. THADDEUS ALMANAC'S SCIENTIFIC PROPOSAL.

A CHRISTMAS STORY.

A YOUNG man, short, and so muffled in an ulster that you could not see his face, pushed into a small, empty corner in the entry of a very large store and tried to stamp some of the snow off his feet. It was snowing heavily, and everyone that càme in was white and wet. The young man got into the crowd again and pushed through the swinging door into the store. It was impossible to go where you wished without tremendous shoving, and impossible to stop without clinging to the woodwork; for there was only one day more to buy Christmas presents, and the whole town seemed to have gathered to do its shopping in this one store.

The young man at last managed to squeeze through to one of the counters, and to keep himself from being brushed away by gripping the edge of the counter. Behind it, a long row of women was flourishing yards of every colored ribbon in the faces of bewildered customers. While he waited, he turned down his overcoat collar from a commonplace but pleasant countenance. Pretty soon a good-looking young woman, with hair like untwisted rope, came to him and put some red ribbon and a piece of paper into a diminutive elevator, which she sent up with a click. Then she wrote in a little book and said to the young man without looking at him, " How many yards? What color?"

" I don't want any ribbon," he answered.

"Wrong counter.   What are you doing here?"

"Admiring you."

The girl looked up and smiled.

"What *do* you want?" she said, arranging her frizzly hair.

"Where is the phonograph department?"

"Basement: take the elevator: seven aisles down," she said, relapsing into her tired, business-like air.

But she brightened again for a second, when he bade her good-bye with a mischievous smile.

It was not from any philanthropic desire to brighten shop-girls' lives that Thaddeus Almanac smiled to the ribbon girl and chatted with the young woman in the phonograph department.   He had an inborn liking for young women who could be suspected of prettiness, and it was natural for him to try to be agreeable to them.   But with the young woman for whom he had the most decided liking, to whom he wished to be particularly pleasant, he was, curiously enough, always shy.   There was no accounting for it.   He could never express himself satisfactorily, even if intelligently, to her.   When he was in her presence he was always uncomfortably embarrassed; but when he was not with her, he always realized that he could be happy only with her.   No amount of practising did him any good.   He could easily be glib with Fifine, his mother's French maid; but he never should be able to tell Jean Barrington that he loved her.   It was all the more unfortunate, too, that he felt sure that he could get along all right, if he were once engaged.

Thaddeus knew that there was another man who admired Jean, and this knowledge made him the more anxious and determined to bring matters to a decisive point. To be sure, he thought this other man an idiot, but he was not quite certain that Jean agreed with him, though he sincerely hoped so. It was not hard to decide to ask Jean to be his wife, but it was very hard to ask her.

He wanted to inquire of every married man he knew how he had proposed: he read sensational novels with avidity, solely to see how the hero courted the heroine; and he invested in a most interesting little treatise on "How Men Propose." But all the men given as examples were heroes of fiction; so this did not seem to help him any, for he was real, and not a hero of fiction. He felt he could never do it as they did.

He thought of being injured, and asking Jean while she was nursing him back to health; but then he felt sure that his mother would be in the room. To send a cablegram from Paris, confessing his love, seemed feasible; and Thaddeus had almost decided to go to Europe for this purpose, when a new idea came to him. One day, Jean said casually that she was crazy for a phonograph; she had a magnificent collection of autographs, mostly of authors, now she must have a collection of their voices.

Thaddeus decided that a phonograph would be just the thing for him to give her for Christmas. Mrs. Almanac told him that she thought it was perfectly proper for him to make her a present, and that very afternoon he went to Lordan Macy's to buy one.

After ordering the phonograph, Thaddeus proceeded direct to the Barringtons'. He had decided that he had better ask her permission to give her a Christmas present, for she might have different ideas on the subject from his mother. He knew that it would be very hard to ask her; and he knew that he never should have the courage, unless the conversation happened to give him an unavoidable opportunity. He also knew that he was totally unable to contrive an opportunity.

As he was well known at the Barringtons', and as a large express bundle arrived at the same time with him, the maid neglected to take in his card. So when he went into the large parlor unannounced, there was Jean sitting in a low chair, gazing abstractedly into the fire, unaware of his presence. She looked so pretty, and he was stricken with such a stage-fright on coming thus unexpectedly upon her, that he stood still, staring at her. And probably he would have stood that way a long time, if she had not felt him looking at her, and turned round, exclaiming, "Thad —!"

A cold shiver ran up Thaddeus's back.

Then she jumped up and said, "Mr. Almanac, how do you do? I was just thinking about you."

She was slightly embarrassed herself, but she need not have been, for Thaddeus was as much transported by delight as if an angel had suddenly appeared and said, "We have been praising you in Heaven." Probably more.

After they had both sat down, Miss Barrington went on, with a remark that hardly "geed" with her other, "I have been wishing again for a phonograph :

that is what I was doing when you came. But oh, I talk so much about it, that everyone will think I am never satisfied."

" Of course," said Thaddeus; "oh, I mean, not at all: of course not."

This afternoon he hardly cared what he said. She had been thinking of him. She had called him Thad. He congratulated himself all the way home on having bought the phonograph. It was the most fortunate idea of his life.

The next morning Thaddeus went up to his room right after breakfast, fixed the phonograph on the table, and was ready for his task. He stood in front of the phonograph a long time. He had thought it would be very easy to tell his love to a wax cylinder, but really it was almost as hard as to tell it to Jean herself. But then he knew no one could resist so romantic a proposal, and this thought made him start out bravely. He had said only a few words when he heard someone knock at the door, and come in. It was Fifine, who had come to dust the room. She looked very pretty in a pink gown, set off with her spotless white cap and apron; so Thaddeus talked a minute or two with her, before going out. Of course, he could not go on with his work while she was there, so he left the phonograph on the table, and waited until after lunch to finish the message.

It was, as Thaddeus had thought, the custom of the Barringtons for each of the family to have his Christmas presents in his own room. Jean used to go to bed early, and put her head under the covers, so that she should discover nothing. Then her mother and her father would go to her room, and spend all their energy and love in arranging the gifts of this only child. Nora, Jean's maid and often her confidant, had particular instructions repeated carefully every Christmas Eve, to wake Jean as soon as she got back from early Mass: then the two young women enjoyed the presents together.

On Christmas morning Jean waked at Nora's first knock and sprang up to open the door. She paused with a little scream of delight at an opera cloak spread over the chair by her bedside. She put it on quickly, and opened the door with a shout of " Merry Christmas." Her feet peeped out from the bottom of the pink silk robe, there was white fur round her neck, and lace escaping under the sleeves at her wrist.

Busily one new treasure after another was opened and exclaimed over and tried on. It was at least half an hour before Nora discovered the phonograph in a corner. She lugged the square, brown box over before the fire and said, "What's this, Miss Jean?"

" I don't know," said Jean, looking up from a manicure-box in tortoise-shell and turquoise: "it doesn't look interesting. You open it."

"Why, what can it be?" she went on, when Nora had taken off the top.

"It beats me," said Nora.

" I, believe it's a sewing machine."

" So it is," agreed Nora; "this spout's where you pour the oil in."

After a little examination she said, " But it's a mighty queer sewing-machine."

"Well, what can it be?" asked Jean, becoming interested and getting down on the floor.

Both young women sat staring blankly at each other and at the machine. At last Jean got up, went to the hall door, and called, "Mama! Mama!"

A voice responded from the distance, and in a few moments Mrs. Barrington appeared, coming down the hall in a wrapper.

"Oh, Mama," cried Jean: "Merry Christmas. I have the funniest present. Come and see what it is."

Just as her mother got to the door, Jean clapped her hands and cried, "I know. It's a phonograph!"

"Of course it is," said her mother when she saw it, for she had seen one before.

Jean was no less anxious than Nora to set the thing going, now they knew what it was. But none of the three could start it. Jean was afraid to experiment with it much; but she studied over the apparatus carefully, while her mother went to examine the other presents. Once Jean touched a spring, and a quick buzzing made them all jump. At last Nora said, "Who is it from?"

After some search the card was found in the cover. Jean delightedly expressed her appreciation of Mr. Almanac's kindness; but she smiled so much that she would have had to say a good deal more to express her feelings.

"He's awfully good," said Nora, reminiscently.

Jean was interested in a newly discovered lever at one side of the phonograph. So it was a little while before she asked who was awfully good.

"Mr. Almanac," answered Nora; "he gave Fifine a lovely present. It is an opera-glass bag."

"Who is Fifine?" asked Jean, absently.

"Mr. Almanac's maid. I mean his mother's maid. I saw her at church this morning. She's French."

"An opera-glass bag?" said Jean; "that was nice."

"Well," explained Nora; "Fifine was not sure whether it was an opera-glass bag, or a slipper bag to take to parties."

Jean had to give up making the phonograph go; and she decided to wait till dinner-time, when Mr. Almanac should be there, for he and his mother were to dine with the Barringtons.

There was a large party for dinner, among them Almanac's rival. Thaddeus had determined to watch Jean's behavior closely to see what she thought of his communication. But there was no need of this. As soon as he was in the room, Jean hurried up to him.

"Merry Christmas!" she said; then in a lower voice, "oh, it was so sweet of you."

"Then you did not think I was forward?" said Thaddeus, as his confidence came to him in a great burst of joy.

"Of course not," she said, smiling; "you knew it was just what I wanted."

"Then you accept—"

"Accept!" she interrupted; "certainly. I am so happy."

Just then somebody came to speak to Jean, and they were separated. Almanac felt that Jean could be no happier than he was. She had accepted him, they understood each other,— his joy was complete; and at the same time he had a satisfactory conviction that he never should be shy again.

An old uncle had the honor of taking Jean to dinner. She and Thaddeus sat on opposite sides; and they cast delightful glances at each other. Thaddeus, indeed, could not keep his eyes off Jean. He did not know whether he had light or dark meat of the turkey.

A bachelor cousin at the far end of the table called down to Jean to ask what presents she had received. As she went through the long list, Thaddeus noticed, with alternate doubt and satisfaction, that she did not mention the phonograph; but at the end she said that there was another perfectly lovely one, which they were all to see before long. She smiled over at Almanac, whose heart suddenly fell; the proposal roll was the only one that had been used; could she be going to announce the engagement in so public a way? Then he realized that she had probably been filling new rolls all morning.

When the fruit and nuts had been put on, the butler staggered in with the phonograph and put it on the end of the table, before Mr. Barrington. There was silence.

" This," said Mr. Barrington, " is a phonograph. It was presented to my daughter Jean by a friend of hers, and of mine."

Everybody looked at everybody else. Jean looked at Thaddeus, who grew crimson. This must be the announcement. An uncle, who was probably in the secret, got up and said, " I propose the health

of Mr. Thaddeus Almanac; and may he have a
Merry Christmas and a Happy New Year."

There were mild and desultory cheers, and Thaddeus saw his mother beaming at him.

Then Mr. Barrington went on:

"Unfortunately, as no directions came with it,
none of us know enough about the phonograph to
make it go. Therefore we have had it brought
here in order to have Mr. Almanac run it for
us."

Thaddeus suddenly felt giddy; his lips turned
white. Mr. Barrington rose and invited him to the
head of the table. He feebly stood up and faltered,
"I don't know how to work it myself."

Then he tried to laugh.

"I do," said his rival, jumping up.

"There's no roll in it," cried Thaddeus.

"Oh, yes; there is," said his rival.

Thaddeus caught hold of the table. Then he saw
Jean smiling at him. After all, though a public
proposal would be embarrassing, there was nothing
so dreadful in it. He pulled himself together. The
rival started the machine.

Everyone listened, including the butler and the
maids. A sharp click was heard; then Thaddeus
braced himself in his chair and looked at Jean. It
seemed an hour before the machine said anything.
Thaddeus thought perhaps this was a blank roll,
and was almost sorry. After all it would be
glorious to triumph before his rival. But his
meditations were cut short by a distinct metallic
voice from the head of the table. It was not exactly
like Thaddeus, but everyone knew that it was

trying to be; and this is what the brazen Thaddeus said :

"Miss Barrington,— I wish I could call her Jean naturally,— first permit me to offer you a very Merry Christmas. But at this early hour, of what I hope will be the happiest day of our lives for both of us, at a time when I know you are alone, I wish to offer you something else. You must have noticed my admiration for you, you must have noticed that I look upon all other women with indifference, you must have noticed that you are the only— Ah ! *bon jour ! ma belle Fifine ! Que tu es très jolie, ce matin ! Fifine, demain sera Nöel. Ce nuit—*"

But Thaddeus did not wait to hear what else the phonograph said.

Luther W. Mott, '96,
and Louis How, '95·

GOD, MAN, AND THE DEVIL.

ALL Gregory Emerson's friends said that, some day, he would make a name for himself in the world. Indeed, this was not to be doubted, for Gregory himself had so decided before graduating from Harvard, half a dozen years ago. When the time came to think as to what particular line he should win his laurels in, it did not take the young man long to make up his mind. Business was rather vulgar, Gregory thought; medicine was such dirty work; in politics you had to mix with such common people; to be a millionaire it seemed necessary to have a million dollars; so that, really, to a fellow with Gregory's family tree (you know, the Emersons are an old Beacon-street family), literature was the only path open which led to distinction.

Gregory had not been especially bright at college, but then, as he had quite sagely remarked to his guardian, what difference would it make in after life whether he got A's or E's in Semitic History, or Fine Arts, or the Theory of Æsthetics? He was not without training in writing, for he had taken, I think, English A, B, and C, and had been official scorer at one or two class base-ball games. After his decision, he wondered why he had hesitated about becoming one of Boston's staple products — a great author.

So Gregory bought a new desk, began to call his former parlor his "study," and told his friends that he was going in for literature. When this was generally known, invitations began to pour in upon the new writer, his opinions were courted on every subject, and the *Sunday Herald* called him " a talented young literary man."

After a couple of months spent in carefully observing the habits of all the writers that he knew, Gregory thought that he was ready to write a book. What this book should be was a matter of considerable importance. On careful deliberation, a philosophical work seemed to have unusual advantages; it would be something you would praise because you would not understand it, and then he could be so very mysterious when asked about it. Finally, three months after commencing work, he had arrived at the period after the title of the book. Then Gregory, in strict confidence, told a reporter that his forthcoming work was to be entitled " God, Man, and the Devil."

This was in the next morning's paper, and, in a very few days, the new book was the talk of the town. The *Globe* said it would appear in the fall; the *Herald*, that Longmans, Green & Co. would publish it in the spring; the *Transcript* man was informed that Mr. Emerson would soon leave for Palestine, where he would spend several years in research and study; and that his book, when published, would make the philosophical sensation of the nineteenth century.

About two years after reading this notice, I thought I saw Gregory in a crowded *café chantant* in Paris, but as I heard he was in Jerusalem all that year, I certainly must have been mistaken.

Emerson returned to Boston just at the right time. There were no English actors or Indian princes in town, so that undivided attention could be given to dining and wining the most prominent philosopher of the day. He accepted an invitation to lecture on " Philosophy as I Have Found It " at Cambridge, but was prevented by sudden illness. The Authors' Club invited him to become a member, letters from publishers came at every mail, and, to crown all, a well-known soap manufacturer offered him five thousand dollars to write a short note, saying that the philosophy of his soap was that " it floats."

The change of climate affected his health so that he was unable to work for six months, and then his eyes gave out, hindering him very much.

At last it was authoritatively stated that " God, Man, and the Devil " would be out, November 1, 1892. The furore this announcement created was something unprecedented. One magazine printed an editorial to the effect that the book would deal Christianity a blow from results of which it could never recover. *The Critic* had a note from a Boston clergyman, saying that, on the contrary, the book would take a place among Christians side by side with the Bible. At Harvard a prominent young history professor affirmed that the whole work was not original — was founded on an old myth — and would have lectured on the subject had anyone gone to hear him. I read in *Truth*, which I picked up in a barber shop, you know, that " God, Man, and the Devil " was not a philosophical treatise, but simply a *fin de siècle*, Midway Plaisance novel.

Many ladies asked Gregory not to refer to them in his book, while quite as many hinted strongly that they would not at all mind being mentioned.

About the middle of October, Emerson left Boston, saying that he expected to spend three or four days at Tuxedo visiting. He did not go to Tuxedo, nor could any traces of him be found even by the detective his guardian employed. That the public might not be disappointed, some literary friends agreed to look after his book, which, even if he were dead to the world, would remain as an eternal memorial of Gregory Emerson. On looking in his study, in the large drawer of the desk they found a number of sheets of paper. They were all blank save the upper one; on it was written in large letters, "God, Man, and the Devil." That was all.

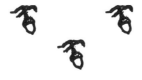

HARVARD TYPES.

I.— THE MOODY MAN.

WHEN I first met him I thought he was home-sick. That was about the fifth week of his Freshman year; the cream of the new life had been skimmed off, and comparisons between home and college were naturally rising to the surface. This might have made him fretful and staringly moody. But he was not melancholy; he was sometimes very alert and jolly. So I can remember one evening, when we sat at the same table, that he twisted every one of my sentences into some grotesque shape; nor could I possibly keep up in counterbalancing his skilful modelling. He could be essentially funny. Indeed, the words he said were not particularly witty, nor did they go to make up a quarter of the nonsense. The way he spoke them, the way his eyes, his hands, his whole body spoke them — that was the main attraction of his sentences. I laughed heartily at him that evening in Memorial Hall, and even the solemn neighbors, who never hear or see anything that is done by an unintroduced fellow, had to wipe away their smiles with their napkins.

He got up after he had shuddered down his dessert and slurred along the stone-paved entrance. He offered me a cigarette. I don't remember ever seeing him without one, except when he rushed for a nine o'clock recitation, a thing he invariably had to do. I accepted his offer, and as we reached the street, he begged me to come to his room. I noticed that his mood was changing and thought I might as well go with him and cheer him up. We climbed to his room — a low, cosy den on Prescott street — and he lit his candles.

"I feel like candles tonight," he said. Then he threw himself on his lounge and looked into the fire.

"Did you see the game today?" I asked, after an awkward pause.

"Hm, hm," he mumbled. He had not heard me at all. His eyes grew as dead as his body; all the soul had left them. His cigarette smoked feebly and then went out. I took up a magazine, trying to read, but looking at him every now and then.

"Poor fellow," I thought, "he's terribly home-sick."

But slowly I found out I was mistaken. He often had those moods and revelled in them. As time went on, he coddled his weakness more and more, till he became unbearable to a great many fellows. Few cared to associate with a man who would not speak for half-hours at a time, and then burst into some passionate appeal, or recite "The Ancient Mariner," to the last light of a candle and with a distant voice. He grew unpopular, and with his unpopularity his weakness increased. He cut all moral lacing, and watched his helpless spirit with delighted interest as it hunched its weak backbone.

His very clothes seemed to express this trait. They hung from his shoulders in a limp way, the whole fellow looking as though he had been suspended a few inches from the ground and was dangling there. Often when I have watched him come down the plank walk in the autumn wind, it seemed to me as if he were rather blown along than walking.

And then he might all at once again pluck up energy and look neat and act neatly. He could have done an extraordinary amount of work if he had only tried. He certainly was not dull, and his strong musical instinct might have made him prominent in his class. But he did not care. He lived for himself, delighting in his selfish mood, scraping through his college courses with C's and D's. He did not want a gilt-edge degree; he wanted to pass, that was all.

I had not seen him for some time, and so I went round to his room a few nights after the hour examinations.

"Come ahead, Landor; let's go into town," I proposed. "It's only seven o'clock now and we can get tickets to some good play."

"Stay a few minutes," he said. "The fire's glowing nicely. Lie down and I'll play for you. I feel just like it."

He blew out his lamp; there was only the glow from the hearth to show the outlines of his many pictures.

"There's nothing like soft light," he almost whispered. "All modern illumination be hanged, and modern invention, too." He threw his cigarette into the fire. "I wish we were back in the days of stage coaches, and periwigs."

He sat down at his piano and began to improvise. It was in the tempo of a minuette, sweeping along with the stateliness of old-time and other days. But suddenly a sad melody seemed to grow in the base. It climbed higher and higher, till it covered the melody of the dance and subdued it to an accompaniment. Now came a curiously wild part: snatches of songs, love songs, drinking songs, parts of sonatas, nocturnes, were mingled and blended. At last he burst into the *Marseillaise*, and ending with a clear, round harmony, he wheeled about his stool, planted his heels on the carpet and looked me square in the face.

"Where did you say you wanted to go tonight? My mind is torn; I can't patch up my thoughts, so let's see something senseless. What can we see? — Do you know my hour exams. turned out a horrible failure. I started my fire two days before they came around and I got to thinking. I dreamt away almost all of two evenings and of two boxes of cigarettes. I was thinking of all the things I might have done and didn't do. You see, that's a good deal to think about. Last night I received my last mark — it put me into a deliciously sad mood. I could have cried had I been a crocodile. But look here, I'm wasting your time, our time. It's half-past seven. We'll go to a variety show."

He had jumped across the room and rushed on his coat, before I could get up from the lounge. As he stood in front of the fire waiting for me to get ready, I could see how scratched with wrinkles his forehead, how undecided his mouth was — it seemed to laugh and cry at the same time.

"Let's go," he said; "and after the performance I feel like getting very drunk."

Edward G. Knoblauch, '96·

II.— THE "PAPER" SPORT.

In the first place, his name is usually **Bilkins** or Snilkins, or something like that, and there is nothing at all to compare him with. It is not even wholesome to think of him in the same thought with that wonderful thing, the real true sport, who is a jolly good fellow and everything that is charming, even if he is the sort of a bird the authorities will not willingly let live.

Bilkins is a little, a very little, wiser than the fellow who comes to Harvard for the rather purposeless purpose of having a royal fine time, and that alone, but he is a vast deal more stupid than the easy-going, idle chap who barely manages to scrape through.

The only pronounced thing about Bilkins is the fact that his abilities are not at all pronounced. He is usually a product of the icy atmosphere of New England, for somehow neither the children of the South nor of the rampant and radiant West lend themselves easily to the hectic "forcing" process that seems necessary for the production of a full-fledged Bilkins. Be that as it may, the miserable little rogue early in his college career gets head over heels in debt to all the tradesmen round-about for paltry little sums, but more than he can afford to owe. The mean part about it all is that these little bills are also, generally speaking, more than his poor old father can easily manage to pay, since his by no means elaborate income is already stretched to keep a roof over a not too diminutive progeny of little Bilkinses up in Bangor somewhere.

What I dislike about Bilkins is that he has so frequently an odious air of having been up all night. At such times, pink-lidded and carelessly dressed, he will rush madly into Foster's for a cup of chocolate while the old bell is clanging to "nine-o'clocks," and then, standing there, he will sip his drink, imparting to the whole somehow a ludicrously rakish air, so that we wonder who this desperate *décadent* is whom indescribable things have prevented from an earlier rising.

Also it is Bilkins who, on any and every college celebration, is the pernicious and inveterate silly little monster, who fuddles himself in public with such shocking ease from a pocket-flask, and who later shouts, " Harvard," and sings naughty songs in bar-rooms, and other lairs of the childless world.

It is Bilkins — the effulgent donkey — who, when he goes home for the shorter recesses, fairly astonishes the gillies of his native heath by the gorgeousness of his waistcoat and the profusion and richness of his elaborate haberdashery. And it is Bilkins, too, who some fine morning vanishes surprisingly from college, while his laundress, and his tailor, and his shoemaker, and his other miserable creditors, are, I fear, a long while a-settling their little accounts.

On Saturday night it is Bilkins who sits in the front row of the " Black Crook," and attracts the pretty chorus girls with outrageous ogles and delusive smiles, and who afterwards loafs with an almost irritating swagger into the Adams House, where he plants himself, a tittering monument of folly, among his kind, and discusses with them, over his cream pie and beer, ostentatious stories of his origin and his luck at cards, and his luck with women, and his luck with this, and his luck with that, filling his important little person meanwhile with the cheapest of cheap food and drink.

It was here that I, wandering in the other evening, found him. I don't know why the deuce he should have smiled his silly smile at me. I'm no "sport," and he knows it far better than I do. Still I went over and shook the paw of this Bilkins and that of his friend, Gilkins, who was so promptly introduced, and I sat down with them for a little while.

"I shouldn't advise you to smoke that weed, old man," commenced this Bilkins as I pulled out a cigar; "here are some fine cigarettes, Richmond Straight, you know. What is that you're drinking? A cocktail! Say, you're quite the sport, aren't you? Well, every man must have his fling. Ah, you sly puss, *I* saw you at the 'Black Crook.' You needn't deny what brought you there. Ah, old fellow, when will you learn that the whole thing doesn't pay? Say, but that was quite the cute peach at the left end of the first line. Did you notice? Quite the enormous fine." And so forth and so forth.

I sat there and listened while he and his friend Gilkins babbled to one another of all things known in a college world; until at length, by easy stages, they approached that one topic dear to the Bilkins heart — the question of ancestry.

Who shall say how it all came about, or how they sat there discussing and wrangling until the blue blood of all this New England aristocracy seemed to course that night in the sluggish veins of Bilkins and of Gilkins.

"Of course," said Bilkins to me, emerging for the moment from a contemplation of a distaff, "you cannot appreciate. You, you know, are merely a New Yorker." Then he plunged back again with redoubled fury into his genealogical labyrinth.

As I listened to these youths that fearful evening, I wondered this and I wondered that, and while I was wondering, perhaps I wondered not so much why Bilkins should have even dreamed of coming to Harvard, as why after coming he should have even dreamed of remaining. And I ended by wondering why I wondered at all,— the *raison de plus* being really so very obvious.

And I was roused from all my idle meditation by the hasty departure of Bilkins to catch the last car. For, be it known, this Bilkins is thrifty even in his dissipations, and while swallowing a tailor's bill a yard long, will strain at the price of a herdic back to college.

And so I was left alone. For of course Gilkins went with Bilkins. For Gilkins considers Bilkins the very funniest of clever men, and, with the possible exception of himself, the very finest gentleman in all New England.

John Mack, Jr., '95.

III.— THE COLLEGE BELLE.

The College Belle is never a Cambridge girl. Ever since 1635 she has annually come "out of the

everywhere into the here," for little visits of nine or
ten months.   She usually comes, moreover, at the
request of a despairing mother whose own many
daughters are *not* belles.   The despairing mother
feels toward her guest very much the same gratitude
that during the latter part of August might be called
forth by something new in fly-paper.   In a word,
when the College Belle is visiting in Cambridge,
Hollis Holworthy and his friends positively flock to
the house at which she is staying, whereas, when
she is not there, they sometimes leave their cards
on Friday afternoons or on Thursday evenings.
The College Belle possesses all the objectionable
and a few of the desirable qualities of that creation
whom European readers of Mr. Henry James like
to think of as "*the* American girl."   She is pretty,
of course.   No girl who is not can ever be attractive to very young — or very old — men.   She likewise has an intelligence.   Her beauty, however, is
more than ordinarily ephemeral, and her mind a
wayward thing.   In fact, Hollis Holworthy, who
has all the inherited discretion of a Boston patrician,
assures me that her mother — whom he has never
met — is an abundant, pillowy person with a moustache.   Moreover, I do not think that in his most
imaginative moments he has ever considered the
possibility of a meeting between the College Belle
and his sisters, Mildred and Gwendolyn Holworthy.

However that may be, he himself enjoys meeting
her at church and walking home with her, and
calling her by her first name, and talking to her in
the dining-room or library, lest they be disturbed
were they to go into the drawing-room.   Since it

might perhaps be unkind to call the Belle exces-
sively bad form, I shall content myself with saying
that she successfully realizes the paradox of being
a " summer girl" all the year round. She is often
spoken of as having " ready tact." Yet when one
sees her at bay, carrying on separate conversations
with two law students, a Senior, a Junior, and at
the same time finding leisure to roll her eyes at a
Freshman somewhere across the room, she im-
presses one as a person of striking ability rather
than a person of tact.

" I have a bone to pick with you," she called to
me the other evening, as I made my way behind a
little knot of men talking to her in Brattle Hall.
This is the Belle's favorite method of beginning a
conversation, which, like all her conversations, con-
sists of the merest chaff and the oscillation of two
large eyes.

Later, when I stood before her and penitently
asked what I had done, she nipped a rose-leaf between her lips and reproachfully taxed me with
having " cut" her in the Square that morning.
We played all sorts of allegretto and scherzo varia-
tions on this simple theme, and could have gone on
indefinitely, had not the Belle gently dropped me
for some '97 men who just then came up. Of
course, I was annoyed for the moment, until I
remembered how incessantly (if the Belle ever reads
poetry) the refrain of Tennyson's " Brook" must be
running through her head.

C. M. Flandrau, '95.

IV.—"HOLLIS HOLWORTHY."

The expression, "the typical Harvard man," is a form of damnation most frequently used by persons of facetious inclination who have never been to Harvard. They profoundly apply that rhythmical phrase in the same breath to a stupendous variety of young American males. In their jocose idea it seems to hit off cleverly, alike, the vapid youth from anywhere, in British garments and accent, the self-contained Bostonian, whose *pince-nez* straddles his aristocratic nose with well-bred hauteur, and the handsome man with much money, much manner and the reputation of being fast. These and many more are constantly alluded to as "the typical Harvard man," when in truth that complex ideal has fortunately never been realized. Of course, Harvard has her types,— the sport, the grind, the swipe,— those saviours of college journalism bear witness of this fact. But no one of these types is the type, and it is to be devoutly hoped that the Alma Mater will never nourish that necessarily monstrous being who will combine the aggregate qualities of the sport, the grind, the Glee Club man, the literary man, the athletic man, the aimless man, and so on through the list of fellows one knows so well, in such a way that he may justly claim the title of "the typical Harvard man."

A moment or two ago, while biting the end of my pencil and waiting for inspiration, I happened to glance out of the window and saw Hollis Holworthy strolling through the yard. He was going to a lecture in the Museum, and he was late, but his narrow Russia leather shoes moved no more rapidly along the walk on that account, for one of the first articles in Holworthy's creed is, "There is nothing so vulgar as haste." If he were to run, he might become warm and even dishevelled, and who, pray, has ever seen Hollis Holworthy warm and dishevelled?

As he walks leisurely along, everyone worth knowing in college nods pleasantly to this rather vague, gentlemanly, and altogether charming upper-classman, and all the rest — the ones who are not worth knowing — wish that they might do the same. But the fact that they don't know him, and are never likely to, doesn't cause them to dislike him, as is frequently the case with certain men at Harvard. For Hollis Holworthy has no enemies.

I have said that he was a rather vague person, and by that I mean that it is extremely difficult to discover his precise relation to college life, and to label him this, or the other, as one is in most cases able to do. For he is never athletic enough to be an athlete, nor sporty enough to be a sport. He writes not, neither does he sing; in fact, the most definite things that one can say of him are, first, that he comes from Boston, and secondly, that he is good looking, good company, and good form. He has been known to belong to cricket elevens, and may occasionally be seen doing the picturesque on a cool, shady tennis court with a pretty girl. In May and June you are also liable to come upon two of him canoeing on the Charles. You, in all proba-bility, are purple and on the verge of sunstroke, but

Hollis Holworthy was never more unruffled and attractive than he is at that moment, as he sits there in his immaculate boating flannels, waving you a suave greeting. It is worth while to note that his recreations are never violent and invariably admit of a delicate-colored shirt and snowy trousers of some kind. He doesn't row and he doesn't run,— both of which facts incline one to the horrible suspicion that, beautiful as he is, he doesn't undress well.

No one has ever mistaken Holworthy for a sporty man — not that he is in any way an unsophisticated person, his acquaintance is too large for that. Furthermore, he plays a fair game of poker, and at social functions of a distinctly undergraduate character he is apt to get drunk. But it is not his nature to do these things, it is merely his scrupulous observance of "form."

Hollis isn't a very clever boy. Perhaps the most acute thing about him is his thorough awareness of the superfluity of being clever. Never, in the entire course of his monotonous existence, has he consciously attempted to make a bright remark, and yet he is quite as well satisfied as any, and much more satisfied than some of his acquaintances who converse in feeble epigrams.

"There's Hollis Holworthy," said a Cambridge girl to me at a tea not long ago. "Do you know, he's one of the few men who don't look abominably in those frock-coat-Mother-Hubbard-bath-robe garments that all you youths are wearing now."

She was one of those jolly old Cambridge girls who have danced at Class Days since the later seventies, and who are fond of nibbling macaroons in corners, and dissecting the Cambridge world for your entertainment.

" Good-looking chap," I mused perfunctorily — one is often called on to say this of Holworthy.

" Who would think that my foolish heart used to flutter and beat faster whenever I saw him," she continued, playing coquettishly with her coffee-spoon.

I conveyed to her the fact that she interested me.

" He affects all girls that way — for a while," she said, " and then — I don't know what it is, exactly — but — well — they get to be able to talk and walk and dance with him, and at the same time feel quite unmoved. I think that we must outgrow him. His mental calibre doesn't seem to expand with his years. I think he stops receiving new impressions long before he comes to college. A girl soon gets to know all he has to say on any subject, but she never remembers any of it until he begins to tell it to her over again. The " —

" Oh, come, come, that's rather rough," I interrupted, feeling called upon to defend one of my special admirations.

She paid no attention to me, however, and went on with :

" The fact that his people are one of those unfortunate American families with traditions may have something to do with it. They're simply stewed in traditions, — Charlemagne, William the Conqueror, and — that sort of thing — direct, unbroken line, you know — all in a gilt-edged book with red leather covers and an intoxicated unicorn on the outside. Oh, they've got traditions, those Holworthys.

"But you won't go away with the idea that I don't like him. Now, will you?" She looked a trifle alarmed. "Because I do, ever so much. He's a sweet thing, and I'm going to bow to him. There. How nice, he's coming over. Don't look conscious — oh, well, he wouldn't notice even if you did."

C. M. Flandrau, '95.

AN UNCONVENTIONAL DETECTIVE STORY.

NEVER before had there been such excitement in the American National Bank of Denver as there was about noon on March 12, 1894. The clerks were talking in great excitement, without paying the usual attention to the great ledgers which lay wide open on the desks. A busy-looking young man with a note-book and pencil is running round with studied bustle, interviewing anyone who will be interviewed. Everyone stops talking as the massive doors swing open, and a short, middle-aged man strides rapidly into the room. He looks at everyone at once and says to everyone at the same time, "I am Sprague,— Socrates Sprague of Pinkerton's. Where is Mr. Jonesandsmith? He sent for me."

The chattering has ceased, all the clerks are looking at the great Sprague,— Socrates Sprague. Someone says Mr. Jonesandsmith is in his office, and the detective bows methodically and opens the door on which he sees in gold letters, "President's Room."

In one corner of this room was a desk heaped up with papers, letters, and what not. In front of the desk a revolving chair was a little more than filled by a man with grey hair and red face, who held a copy of the "United States Investor" in his hand, but as it was upside down, it was not, evidently, interesting him very much. He laid it on the desk when he heard the door open, and a man exclaimed,

"I am Sprague,— Socrates Sprague of Pinkerton's. You telephoned for me, I believe. If you'll tell me all the circumstances of the case, I'll capture the robber, or it'll be the first time I've ever been fooled."

Mr. Jonesandsmith seemed comforted, lighted a cigar, tilted his chair back, and started in, giving the other man no chance to get in a word until the story was finished. "Have a cigar?" he began. "No? Well, that's twenty-five cents in my pocket! You see, it was this way. I came down town this morning in my usual spirits and the Seventeenth street cable. I came in here, read the morning's papers, and thanked Heavens I hadn't sold Louis-ville and Nashville short, as I'd been going to do. I wrote a couple of letters and was starting on the third, when I heard an obsequious knock on the door, and said, 'Come in!' expecting to see a beggar, or a minister, or a book agent, or some other obnoxious person. But, instead, a very mild and respectable-looking man opened the door, shut it carefully, and stood waiting for me to ask him to sit down. I did so, and he drew a chair up quite close to me. Putting his hand on my knee, he said in a low voice, 'Mr. Jonesandsmith, I want ten thousand dollars! Now, don't think I'm a crank, for I'm not. I know perfectly well what I'm doing, and I've thought it all over. When I tell you about my plan, you'll see I'm no fool. It is absolutely necessary that I should have this money today. If I don't get it, I might just as well kill myself. Now I don't know of any way to get it except to have you give it to me.'

"Then he stopped, took a little vial of a whitish liquid out of his pocket and went on, 'You see this bottle? Well, there's enough nitro-glycerine in it to blow this whole institution into Heaven or Hell, as the case may be. Don't be foolish, Mr. Jonesandsmith! If you keep perfectly calm, everything will be all right. What I want you to do is to go out to the cashier and give him your check for ten thousand dollars. Tell him you want it in large bills, and then hand it over to me. I will put it in this bag, and you will shake hands with me and walk to the front door with me. You can stand there, and watch me drive off in that buggy you see outside, and then you can give the alarm or do anything you want. You won't see me again, though. If you do this, all's well and good; if not, I'll just drop this bottle on the floor and meet you a few minutes later in another world. I'm going to walk out to the cashier with you, and if you make the least sign to him, or in any way show that anything is wrong, it'll be the last thing you'll do in this world. I see you don't quite understand my scheme, so I'll give you five minutes to think it over in. You need not hope that someone will come in here, for I told the clerks to admit no one, as I had an important appointment with you and could not be disturbed.'

"Then he stopped and sat still for a few minutes, all the time playing with the bottle in a most annoying manner. I don't think I've ever been so uncomfortable in my life, and I've had some pretty tough experiences, too. I looked steadily at him; he seemed calm and desperate. I was quite sure he had told the truth. Ten thousand dollars is a good deal of money, I thought, but then it's a cheap price to pay for living. I felt sure that I could let the cashier know that something was up, so, like a damned fool, I wrote out the check.

"'I'm glad to see that you are taking a sensible view of the situation,' the man said, and walked into the other room with me. The cashier said afterwards that I looked very pale, but he didn't notice it at the time. I started to tell him to seize the man, but I could not talk; my mind was on that bottle of nitro-glycerine. The man took the money, counted it slowly, put it in his bag, and walked to the front door. I thought if I could once get to the door I could watch him and call for help from some passer-by. But as I got to the door, he turned around, said, 'I'll thank you to hold this for me,' and handed me the bottle with the nitro-glycerine in it. Of course, I was so paralyzed with fear lest I should drop it, that I did not move for three minutes, and that's the last I saw of my ten thousand dollars. Now, Mr. Sprague, I want you to catch that man. I'll fix up the reward business all right."

"By Vidocq!" exclaimed Socrates Sprague, "if that ain't the neatest piece of work I've heard of for a long time! Catch him? Oh, yes! I can do it! There's only one man in the country who could put up such a job, and that's Martin O'Melia, alias Jan Zmith, alias Ariel Boggs, alias Ronald Donaldson, alias Tony Von de Van Dresser!"

II.

1. *Lionel Grand, who gave his occupation as character-student and his residence as Denver, being duly sworn, deposed as follows:*

That while he was leaning against a post near the American National Bank, at quarter-past eleven A. M., he saw a man come out of the bank, get into a buggy, and drive off. As he was occupied only in chewing a straw and was accustomed to notice people, he had made a mental Kodak of the man in the short time he saw him. The stranger was tall and middle-aged, with a full grey beard. He wore a derby hat and a dark blue suit and light gaiters. He did not drive very fast on getting into the buggy, but he soon turned a corner and disappeared. The horse was a red roan. On being asked if he could identify the man, he said, without doubt. He had not seen any bag in the man's hand.

2. *Margaret Blessed, spinster, being duly sworn, deposed that:*

While she was walking on Seventeenth street, near Oregon, at 10.45 A. M., a young man furiously driving a white horse in a buggy had almost run over a child that was crossing the street. She had seized the child's arm and pulled her out of danger, after which she had gone into a neighboring house and indulged in hysterics. She had noticed that the young man was very much excited.

3. *Douglas Glass, druggist at Fifteenth and Oregon streets, being duly sworn, deposed as follows:*

About half-past eleven a calm, middle-aged man with a smooth face, dressed in a grey check suit and carrying a small bag, had come in for a glass of vichy. Saw nothing remarkable in his appearance, but had noticed that he wore low shoes, because he put one foot on a chair to tie his shoe-string. Had been surprised that his shoes were clean, because it was very muddy. Therefore, he had gone to the door to look out, after the stranger left, and saw a buggy a little way up the street, with a piebald horse, very hot and sweaty. Supposed the man had gone into the house in front of which the buggy stood.

4. *Napoleon James Marrow, conductor number 2140 of the East Denver Cable Road, being duly sworn, deposed as follows:*

About noon, a common-looking man with a bag had got on car number 1111 at Oregon and Sixteenth. Would never have noticed the man if he had not tried to pass a Canadian dime. Then he observed that he wore high boots, which were very muddy. Thought the man had a full black beard. Did not remember where he got off.

5. *Mrs. Serena Goveney, laundress, being duly sworn, deposed as follows:*

Had set alongside the gentleman that tried to pass the Canadian dime in the East Denver cable car. Knew he had never a bag, for she had been after putting her bundle of clothes on the seat betwixt herself and him. She had discovered that she had no money with her, and the gentleman had paid her fare to keep an old woman from being fired from the cable. She thought he was an Irishman and had red hair.

6. *Ed Or, gripman number 1749, being duly sworn, deposed that:*

He had been running grip car 16, of which 1111 was a trailer, before noon. He had seen nothing whatever of the man in question.

7. *Mary Grey, music teacher, being duly sworn, deposed as follows:*

She had ridden on the East Denver cable about eleven A. M. She had noticed a young man in a blue suit with a derby hat. He was very neatly dressed, with gloves and his trousers turned up. She remembered thinking he looked like an Eastern man, and wondering if he had come from Kansas City. She thought he had a dress-suit case with him. She saw him pay the old Irishwoman's fare, which had heightened her interest in him. They both rode to the end of the line and she thought he had gone down the country road to the right. She knew that he had not gone in the 11.30 horse-car of the extension line, which she herself had just managed to catch.

8. *Sylvester Stanton, assistant starter of the East Denver Cable Road, being duly sworn, deposed as follows:*

He had noticed a very tall man with a high hat get off the cable car and take the 11.30 car on the extension. He thought the man was middle-aged and benevolent looking and had remarked that he carried a flageolet-case.

After this Socrates Sprague of Pinkerton's was unable to follow the clue any farther, for all trace of the stranger whom he had supposed to be the bank robber here disappeared.

Luther Wright Mott, '96,
and Louis How, '95.

WHEN I was in Ireland last summer, I fell in with an Englishman — a sleek little fellow who seemed to have alternate moods of wool-gathering and excitability. He carried about a huge note-book, and when he was not talking or dreaming, he was taking notes. He informed me in a most impressive manner that he had come to Ireland to gather material for a book he was going to write some day, and the title was to be "Why Ireland should be de-Anglicized."

It was in Athlone that I met him, and as we were so near "Sweet Auburn," Oliver Goldsmith's birthplace, he proposed we should take a jaunting-car and spend half a day there. To do this, we had to start early in the morning.

It was a dull drive of five miles, and a veil of rain shut out the landscape. I was almost asleep, but my companion, who was in one of his enthusiastic moods, talked enough for us both. Presently, however, he fell to arguing with the driver on the Home Rule question, and I was forced to wake up to keep peace between them.

"I've a great respect, in fact a great admiration, for you Irish," said the little man most patronizingly to the driver, "but I think you're altogether wrong in this unfortunate question. You imagine, don't you know, that when you get Home Rule, the land is going to flow milk and honey. Now don't you see it's all very ridiculous?"

The driver turned round abruptly, eyed the Englishman contemptuously for one brief moment, and then said, "Get up, Sheela," to the shambling mare. But the Englishman thought he had scored a point.

"The fact of the matter is," he went on in the same strain, "you Irish don't know what you want. Come now, you don't, do you?"

"Faith, then, we do."

"Well, what on earth is it?"

"We don't want *what we've got*," was the sententious answer.

"Humph!" said the little man, sniffing the air. "That's it! That's a fine specimen of your unreasonable Irish reasoning."

"Don't you think there's a good deal to be said on both sides of the question?" I broke in, in the cause of peace. But this pleased neither side.

"Very barbarous, very imaginative, very kindly-hearted — I understand them perfectly," soliloquized the Englishman in a half undertone.

The driver began to hum:

"From mountain and valley
'Tis liberty's rally —
Out and make way for the bold Fenian men."

The Englishman was thereupon irritated. "You haven't a good voice, driver," he remarked; "in fact, it's decidedly bad. You should have it cultivated."

"Me voice is me own, sir," replied the driver. "I'm sorry 'tis not melodjous." And he went on:

"We'll raise the old cry anew,
Slogan and Con Hugh,
Out and make way for the Fenian men."

"If you don't stop that infernal Irish racket, driver, I shall get down and walk."

"'Pon my soul, sir, you're welcome. But the walking's not good this morning, sir. 'Tis wet under foot.

> "We've made the false Saxon yield
>   Many a red battlefield.
> God on our side, we shall do so again."

"Driver, stop the car this minute! Do you hear me? I shall certainly get down and walk"—

But just then the mare shied at a stone, the car lurched to one side, and the Englishman was thrown back violently into his seat.

"If you really would fancy walking, sir, on this ilegant sunshiny morning"—(this was of course sarcastic, for the rain was falling in sheets)—"if you would indeed like to walk, sir, I'll stop the mare. Whoa up, Sheela! But, sir, be careful of the bog-holes—they're hidjous deep, some of 'em, with wather enough in them to drown a dozen Englishmen. Whoa up, Sheela!"

The jaunting-car at last came to a stop.

"And be careful, too, sir," continued the driver with perfect gravity, "be careful when you go by McKenna's shebeen. He keeps a blood-thirsty divil of a dog, that would chew you to rags, if he didn't know you."

The little man winced. Then he said with a snap, "Drive on."

"And you're not going to walk? Dear me, how onreasonable the English are anyway. Faith, they don't know what they want. Get up, Sheela!"

The little man busied himself nervously with his huge note-book and stole a furtive look to see if I was laughing; but I buried my chin in my mackintosh and feigned sleep.

And the rest of the way to Goldsmith's village the driver triumphantly sang his patriotic ditty, exhorting the Saxon to make way for the brave Fenian men.

Coercion has always accomplished a good deal for Ireland!

When, after reaching Sweet Auburn, we had gone into the kitchen of "The Three Jolly Pigeons" to dry ourselves before a rousing turf-fire, the little man said, impressively, "I shall change the title of my book, sir."

"Indeed?" I remarked. "You won't write on 'Why Ireland should be de-Anglicized'?"

"Most decidedly not, sir. I shall write a book favoring the other side of the question."

Townsend Walsh, '95.

ON A PARIS OMNIBUS.

THE large yellow wheels of the Clichy–Odéon omnibus came slowly rattling down the boulevard. The dusty crowd that, desperate and dripping with perspiration, was waiting at the little transfer, rushed frantically into the street and huddled like a flock of sheep round the conductor.

He looked at them condescendingly, puffed out his cheeks, wiped his forehead with his sleeve, and then began slowly, "*Soixante — dix-huit; soixante — dix-neuf, quatre-vingt.*"

A few envied ones got seats. Then, with the same cold-bloodedness, the conductor put up the sign, "*Complet,*" and again began the floppy beat of the horses' feet upon the wooden pavement.

I, both preferring to save my three sous and to enjoy the populace, went up on top. Here I got all the savory smells of the bakeries and cafés, and by looking down on the swarming multitude hurrying restlessly to and fro, I became almost dizzy.

Next to me sat a workman, in a long blouse and with his dinner-pail between his feet. He saw I was tired and exasperated and evidently wanted to cheer me. Several times he looked as if he wanted to say something, but I only turned my back on him. At last, too warm-hearted to be rebuffed in that way, he thrust his hand into his pocket and pulled out a dirty, shrivelled-up tobacco-pouch and cigarette paper. He rolled a cigarette, which without further ceremony he licked and put in my mouth. I smoked it out.

Next to him were two more workmen, with their flushed faces within a few inches of one another, both of them highly excited.

"Well, I tell you, I did see him yesterday," said one.

"You didn't," answered the other.

"I did."

"You didn't."

"I did."

They were just coming to blows when the conductor appeared. The one nearest me looked at the other with infinite scorn and added:

"Well, then, you didn't, and that settles it."

We had now reached the opera. The chestnut trees were in bloom, and the air was filled with their sweet fragrance. At Café Riche all the small marble-topped tables were occupied. Overladen waiters were hurrying and scurrying everywhere, tripped up by their long aprons. All were laughing and talking at the top of their voices, and clinking their absinthe glasses together.

But we rattled past.

The conductor, however, was now in a violent discussion with a woman who refused to pay her hire until her child had finished suckling, not wanting to disturb "*la pauvre chérie qui en a bien soif.*"

Up by the driver was sitting a printer's devil, whistling snatches of popular Parisian ditties and trying to see how far he could spit, and if he could reach the walls of the houses we passed.

Beside him was an enormous yellow straw hat covered with poppies. High on the railing in front

of it rested a pair of small shoes. The skirt pinned
up, so as not to get soiled by the street dust, revealed
a pair of small ankles, covered with little black
stockings, through which we could see little squares
of pink flesh. The railing would often receive an
impatient kick when the priest next to poppies
would raise the pitch of his voice while reading
an endless string of prayers out of a worn
book.

A stout woman, with large red hands covered with
the slimy scales of fish, was greatly taken up with a
piece of chewing-gum which she every now and
then pulled out of her mouth to see if its color had
changed from pink to white.

Fat persons somehow always happen to sit beside
each other, and here, also, fate was cruel, for next
to the fishy woman sat a poor fellow making heart-
rending attempts to extract a sou out of his pocket,
which to him was in a vague somewhere under-
neath his stomach, that hung in helpless folds.

" *Le Figaro — le Gil Blas — le Petit Journal — le
Fi-ga-ro,*" shrieked a newsboy in the shrillest Parisian
tones.

A sigh of despair was uttered by the whole car
when a woman with a baby and a little fellow of
about five appeared at the head of the steps.

A few minutes afterwards, however, the little
expressionless lump of flesh was being energetically
kissed by several of the women, and the little boy
was relating, for the edification of us all, the whole
of his family history.

At Palais Royal we had to stop, the street being
too blocked with furiously swearing drivers and an

excited crowd, for us to advance. I got off and asked one of the mass what was the matter.

"*On croit qu'il y a quelque chose,*" she answered, laughing and shrugging her shoulders.

John Allyne Gade, '*96*.

THE SLEEPING CAR.

LAST summer I was in Paris with my cousin Marie and her mother, when one day I received a telegram from my husband, bidding me meet him in Constantinople on Friday. This was Tuesday, and as it takes nearly forty-eight hours to reach Constantinople even by the fast trains, I had no more time than was necessary to make my preparations. I went at once to get my tickets, and considered myself fortunate in securing a compartment near the middle of the sleeping car, where I would be least disturbed by the jar and rattle of the wheels.

When I told Marie of my arrangement she was horrified by my extravagance.

"Do you mean that you paid for a sleeper all the way to Constantinople," she said.

"Yes; why not?"

"No one but an American would be such a fool! When you get to Vienna you will be the only passenger left in the car, and the conductor will come in and tell you so, and say that you will greatly oblige the management by letting him transfer you to a first-class carriage, and you will have had all your expense for nothing."

"What will you bet I don't go through to Constantinople in the sleeper?" I asked.

"A dozen twelve-button gloves," she replied.

"Done!" said I, as I went to finish my packing.

The train left at twelve the next day. Several people came to the station to see me off and stood talking and laughing, waiting for the train to start.

"Don't forget those gloves," said Marie as the train slowly began to move.

I made myself as comfortable as possible with the pillow I had hired at the stand in the little station, and settled down for a long journey. A large, well-stocked lunch basket made me perfectly independent of the railway restaurants, and I dallied over my luncheon, having nothing better to do. A novel carried me safely through the afternoon, and I went to bed soon after supper, for I wished to be up early in the morning.

When I awoke I arrayed myself in a pretty little yellow morning jacket with black lace trimmings, unpacked my bag and covered every available space with the contents, and, opening the lunch basket, began breakfast. Alas, my too prophetic cousin! Before I had waited ten minutes, the train drew up at a station and a uniformed official appeared in the doorway of my compartment with a couple of assistants. Civilly, and in excellent French, the conductor began just as my cousin had foretold, and explained that they wished to transfer me to a first-class carriage. To which I replied with my sweetest smile and my best Japanese, "Pardon, I do not understand you. What is it you wish?" He looked puzzled and repeated his remark. I, still smiling, did the same. He tried again in pretty fair English, but without result. He consulted his subordinates; then all three disappeared, returning presently with a fourth, who addressed me in German. An Italian followed, and then a Spaniard.

Each time my formula worked to perfection. No sooner were the words out of my mouth than the four vanished. Pray Heaven they don't catch a Jap out there, thought I, for if they do I'm done for. They came back in triumph with a Hungarian, and I was able most comfortably and honestly to repeat my original statement. Puzzled, baffled and disappointed, they looked at each other and again withdrew. Imagine my relief and satisfaction when the train started, effectually preventing my introduction to any other distinguished foreigners who might have been in Vienna that day.

While I dressed and repacked my bag, I composed telegrams to Marie, and after finishing my breakfast, called the porter to make up the bed. He put everything in order, and then, leaning confidentially into the doorway, he remarked in excellent French, " Madam really did that very well. I had the pleasure of observing Madam yesterday at the station in Paris among her friends, and hearing her speak English and also French, the most excellent. As for me, I have a sweetheart in Constantinople, you see, and besides, it was not my affair. Madam and I will both arrive with great pleasure at Constantinople. Can I be of further service to Madam ? "

It was useless to resent the fellow's impudence. We both laughed, and he retired, still chuckling at the discomfiture of the officials.

Willis Munro, '95.

TWILIGHT creeps on. The bustle and excitement of the great city subsides, the sound of hurrying feet and clattering hoofs dies away, the many lights one by one disappear; fainter and fainter grow the cries, till at last they become only whispers borne by the night wind; the shadows advance stealthily and eagerly and slink into their old haunts; the last lingerers find rest, and all is slumbering.

Paris is asleep.

But now came the reveille of Notre Dame. All through the day she had slept, oppressed by long processions of cardinals and priests and choir-boys, by thousands of persons passing hurriedly through her portals, not one of them really caring for her or seeing her beauty; the atmosphere around her was filled with heavy and suffocating incense that insulted her purity; she was scanned curiously, not lovingly; she cared for none of the pomp and magnificence, for neither the scarlet-clad singers nor the virgins dressed in white and wreathed in roses; she could hear their sins and their secrets, blighted hopes and aspirations; but they all tired her, and she slept through them all, as she has slept through it for centuries before.

But in the night, when it was calm and still, and the last sound had become faint, then she awoke,— then Notre Dame of Jehan de Chelles and of Jean le Bouteiller, then the temple of the holy King Louis awoke. And the bells began pealing as they had pealed hundreds of years ago, when they had rung the angelus and the tocsin. Slowly, and mysteriously, and muffled, they rang out into the cold night air.

Gabrielle began slowly and sweetly, but soon Guillaume joined her with his old cracked voice, and Thibauld and the two little ones that were born on Christmas night, and all the rest, and their merry peals made the tower shake and the whole church reverberate. The great organ also joined in the song; three saints, dressed in white and gold, whose garments lay in beautiful folds upon the floor, played upon it with their slender, tapering fingers, which were heavy with rings of gold and costly stones, and they accompanied it with song. The rich old notes were sent down through the aisles and the nave: *Venite, Exultemus, Domino.* . . . And the music swept through the chancel and majestically before the altar, and in and out through the chapels; it filled the whole church with wonderful harmony, and crept out through every crack and crevice into the night air. The moonlight was streaming through all the stained glass windows. As it shone through the south rosette, it filled everything inside with gold, silver and azure. It lighted up the pale marble faces of the saints and knights as they lay stately in their array and mantles, and it filled them with life and vigor, and color came into their faces, and they awoke to life again, and arose. And it reflected the gold upon the holy altar, and the music frisked and played around the columns, who only deigned to nod their finely-chiselled heads. Like muscular giants they held the heavy weights upon their shoulders without flinching an inch or curving their backs. The richly-carved wood, brought from afar by crusaders, filled the air with its dingy fragrance.

Now two streams, one of pure, rich purple and one of bright scarlet, flowed in through one of the windows and lit up the many peering black eyes of the giants.

Notre Dame was awake, quivering and trembling with joy, but no one except her knew or saw what was passing. She had become old, but old age had only made her, like other mothers, more gracious; the stains but added to her beauty.

All the hideous-faced gargoyles and devils and animals were hurrying and scurrying about on her façade, now and then in couples, now in whole swarms perching on the very pinnacles of her turrets and towers. A long row of small devils were slowly scampering down the metal roof of a turret, their nails scratching it harshly; then they gathered their legs under them and quickly coasted down into the dark streets. The eagles spread their wings and flew circling around the porch. But the old devil on the battlement rested his arms on the marble slabs, and his thick-set jaw and thick, flabby lips hung down. Perfectly still he sat, as he was wont to, and gazed out over the roofs and the slumbering city. Then his long, hairy tongue dropped out of his mouth, and he began regularly to lap the iron grating. All the others joined him, and they stretched out their naked arms, rolled their eyes and suckled his breasts, and then hurled themselves down from the low, slanting roof.

But the moon is sinking to rest, its rays are growing dimmer and dimmer; the life of the sleeping
city begins anew.   The bells stop pealing, the
music ceases, the statues become rigid, and one by
one the gargoyles and devils and animals creep
back to their places, and are again gray and still.

Notre Dame is asleep.

John Allyne Gade, '96·

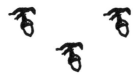

LITTLE SISTER.

A LOVE STORY.

A S Kennard Lockett lived pretty far West, the Harvard authorities allowed him to begin the recess early; and he arrived at home two or three days before Christmas.

The day he got home he spent the morning down town, and returned to the house where he lived about noon. He went to the library and settled himself cosily before the open fire. The room was bright from the reflection of the sun on the snow outside. He lighted a cigarette, crossed his legs, and opened Dickens's Christmas stories. As he was beginning to read "The Cricket on the Hearth," he heard a soft little sound out in the hall. He listened; it was somebody crying.

"Is that you, Little Sister?" he called; "what's the matter? Come down here and see me."

He put the book on the table as he heard slow footsteps out on the stairs: and in a moment a little girl with tangled fair hair and teary eyes came reluctantly into the room.

"Come and talk to me," he said coaxingly; "I have hardly seen you; and it's been so long since we did see each other. You're not too big yet to sit on your big brother's lap, are you?" He lifted her on his knee with one arm and with the other threw his cigarette into the wood fire.

The little sister looked curiously at him. "Don't Papa let you smoke?" she asked.

"Oh, yes; yes, indeed. But I don't smoke when ladies are with me. Where are Mother and Alice?"

"Down town," she said, mournfully; "they wouldn't take me. That's why I was crying." And she sniffled, doubtful whether to begin again.

"Don't you care," said her brother; "I wouldn't want to go. There's nothing so stupid as shopping with women. Probably they are buying your Christmas present, too, and don't want you to see it."

Little Sister brightened.

"I hope it's a dolly house," she said tentatively.

"How do you like Alice?" Lockett asked her.

"I like her. She's just lovely. She lets me see her do her hair. And I like her hair anyhow if it is red. She puts in most a hundred hair-pins — a hundred and seven, I should think. And she has the beautifullest rings and she lets me play with them, and she never says, 'Don't, Helen.' She's goin' to give me one, with a little teeny tiny pearl, out of a oyster."

"Well! that is nice. I'm glad of that. I'm glad you like her."

"I love her," said the little girl with fervor.

Then she fell to rubbing his chin with one hand.

"How nice and smoove you are," she exclaimed. "But why don't you have a beard?"

"I don't let it grow."

Helen eyed him curiously and considered.

"Are you a man now," she asked, "or only a big boy?"

"I'm a man now," he laughed.

She snuggled her head down on his shoulder.

"Then you can get married," she said.

"Why, yes; I can get married."

"I hope you won't, Kennard. 'Cause then you would go 'way, wouldn't you?"

"I probably should," he answered, looking over her head into the fire.

"I hope you won't then. I wish you wouldn't ever have to go 'way."

Alice came into the room before Kennard and his little sister knew it. She was a magnificent red-headed creature. She might have been beautiful, if it hadn't been for her wondrous flame-colored hair, which caused all the rest of her to be insignificant, and made her strikingly handsome.

She came over and put her hand on the little girl's fair head. Lockett got up, and Helen slipped down to the floor, and stood holding by his coat.

"I shall be getting jealous of you, Little Sister," said Alice.

Helen looked up and saw them both smiling in a way she didn't understand. She didn't like it; and when Alice had passed on into the next room to the piano, she climbed silently into her brother's lap.

"What is jalous?" she asked at last.

Lockett laughed. "I am afraid you wouldn't understand it," he said; "Alice was joking."

They talked a great deal about Christmas while Alice played. Little Sister was just taking Lockett up to her nursery to see all her toys, when their mother came in and lunch was ready. "This afternoon," the little girl begged: but after noon her brother was to take Alice to a tea.

That night, as a great and unprecedented favor, Helen was allowed, at her brother's request, to sit up till ten o'clock to see Alice in party dress. The whole family was a strange sight to the sleepy little girl. Her father and her brother were all black with great white U shapes on their breasts. Her mother looked lovely but unnatural in a staid and elegant ball costume of Maltese color. When they sat down to wait for Alice, Little Sister went to Kennard to sit on his knee. He told her to be careful of his shirt front.

"You're not so smoove now," she said, surprised, as she put her finger on his chin.

"I'll be rougher still tomorrow," he told her.

"And then can't you ever get smoove any more?"

"Oh, yes; then I'll shave."

"I want to see you when you do it," she said wonderingly.

Alice was magnificent. Her gown was of a fresh green, with transparent sleeves. One strip of wine-colored velvet ran obliquely round the full skirt. There was a string of beryls in her flaming hair; and one very large one hung from a long gold chain round her neck.

As a maid began to bundle Alice in many soft wraps, Helen's mother said, with painful precision, "Now, Little Sister, you must go up to Jos' Anna."

Helen began reluctantly to kiss people good-night.

"Let me carry her up," proposed Kennard, who had put on his overcoat.

The little girl clung about his neck as he went slowly up the stairs.

"Didn't she look lovely, dear?" he said.

"Yes," answered Helen conscientiously. "But I don't love her any more. You all love her better than me."

"Oh, we all love you, Sweetheart; Alice and all of us. You're the only Little Sister we've got. It was mean that we couldn't sit next to each other at dinner; but you know Alice is a guest, and we must all treat her as nicely as we can. Don't you care. Tomorrow I am coming up to have you show me your dolls. Here we are."

When he put her down, Little Sister reached up her arms and her face to him and he bent down to kiss her.

The next morning when Helen woke she cried to Jos' Anna, "This is Christmas Eve, ain't it?"

"Yeah, deary, dis is Christmas Eve; and de nex' thing we got to do is to choose out a good long stockin'."

That afternoon Lockett spent an hour in the nursery, sitting on the floor, building block houses with his little sister, and being introduced to her many dolls. The little girl was very happy. Suddenly a maid opened the door and cried, "Miss Alice is waiting for Mr. Kennard."

He jumped up. "I must go with Alice," he exclaimed.

"Oh, Alice!" cried Little Sister fiercely. "Alice always spoils everything."

She was going to a party herself that afternoon: and soon after Lockett left, Jos' Anna began to get her ready.

"I 'low Miste' Kennahd is right fond o' Miss Alice," said Jos' Anna in her exquisitely modulated negro voice, as she began to comb the knots out of the fair hair. "I reckon things is go'n' to be" — she paused to think how to express it — "jus' as they mought be."

Helen didn't exactly understand; but she was uneasy. When the time had come for her to go, she was as unhappy and nervous as possible, for Kennard had not come back and her heart was set on his seeing her in her party dress. At last it was dark; and Jos' Anna insisted on starting. Just then a key was heard in the front door.

"It's him!" cried Little Sister, pulling off her cloak as he came in.

She was as pretty in her way as Alice. She had the innocently vain mouth that even a child is lucky to have. Her blonde hair had one wave in it, and was parted in the middle, brushed over her forehead and plainly down on her shoulders, exactly like that of Edward the Fourth. She wore the simplest slip of a white silk frock, with purplish shadows in 't, and blunt white silk slippers without heels.

"You must have a flower," said Kennard with enthusiasm. "I will give you one of Alice's."

Her happy face fell.

"I don't want Alice's flower," she cried fretfully.

"It won't be Alice's, dear. It will be yours, for you. See."

As he took three or four white carnations from the box he held, he said, "You are not jealous of Alice, are you?"

There was the word that Helen did not understand.

Jos' Anna offered him a pin, but he smiled at her

and took his own scarf-pin. He pinned the flowers on his little sister's shoulder.

" I never seen flowe's put on like that afore," protested Jos' Anna : but the effect pleased both the brother and the sister.

Before Little Sister went to bed that Christmas Eve, after all the stockings had been hung on the library mantel, Kennard took her up to his room to watch him shave. She declared it the most fascinating operation she had ever seen,— better than Alice's putting up her hair, ever so much. He was so nice and "smoove" at the end that she kissed him three times on the chin and rubbed her own warm cheek on his cool one. During the proceeding he had been telling her about the early Mass they were going to at five the next morning,— he and Alice, the cook and one of the maids. Helen was in raptures at his descriptions of the yellow-robed priests, the music, the incense, and the small boys in lace with candles in their hands. When they went downstairs she begged her mother to let her go. Her brother was willing to take her, but Mrs. Lockett decided that it was better not, as it might inconvenience Alice.

Christmas morning was lovely. They all had their presents together in the library after breakfast. Helen chafed at waiting : and went wild over her presents. There was the doll-house, and Alice had given her the most beautiful doll she ever saw, with a pink parasol.

She dragged Kennard over to her array of treasures and began to explain everything to him. Just as they had all the furniture out of the doll-house parlor, Alice cried delightedly from a far corner, "Oh, Kennard, you dear boy. How did you know? Come here."

"Alice wants me," he said, getting up.

"Oh, Alice!" cried Little Sister in desperation. "I wish Alice would go 'way."

He came back to her soon, and took her on his knee. "Sweetheart," he said very kindly, "I want you to be very fond of Alice. She and I are going to be married —"

"Then she will take you away —" cried Helen. "I hate her. I do."

She burst out crying and put her head against her brother's breast. He folded his arms round her. But she struggled away from him.

"I think it's mean," she said; "and it's your fault, too, as much as hers."

The engagement was announced at dinner. Little Sister had been comforted, and had been absorbed in the good things to eat. When her father and her different uncles got up in turn, during the dessert, and each made a little speech, she didn't understand what they said. Everyone laughed and drank wine all together; and Kennard stood up at last and looked very red while he tried to speak. Then the women went into the parlor, taking Helen and one small boy cousin.

When the men were heard coming, two of the aunts dragged Alice under the chandelier, where her red hair almost touched the mistletoe. She put her hands over her face, and Little Sister wondered what was going to happen. Suddenly, while everyone talked and laughed, Kennard came running in, pulled away Alice's hands, and kissed her amid clapping from the aunts and the cousins. But Little Sister, sitting by her mother, began to cry softly and put her head down on her mother's lap.

Louis How, '95.

HOW TO GO TO BED.

SLEEP is one of the great pleasures of life; sleepiness is one of the grievous ills that flesh is heir to. How to pass most comfortably from the state of drowsy discontent into the beatitude of complete unconsciousness is a problem in which the whole human race is much concerned, and which, it might be supposed, would, by the end of this nineteenth century, have been definitely solved. Yet no problem of like importance has received less attention from the sages of the world. The only printed piece of advice, so far as I know, about going to bed, concerns a mere detail and has been very justly made a matter of ridicule by the comic papers,— "Don't blow out the gas." Going to bed is not a matter to be so lightly dismissed. After setting forth the requirements for going to bed properly, I shall lay down a few rules as to how to go to bed.

The requirements are three in number: a bedroom, so cold that you can see your breath; a dressing-room, warmed and cheered by a glowing fire; and a broad and soft divan, piled with pillows and placed in front of the fire. With such conditions, there is nothing to prevent you from going to bed luxuriously and in the following manner.

When you begin to feel sleepy, begin to go to bed. Wind up your watch, take off your coat and waistcoat, and hang them over the back of a chair. Next remove your collar and cravat. Then — for deliberateness without deliberation is the secret of my system — sit down and gaze vacantly at the fire.

Don't think; that is disquieting. If you are troubled
with a very active mind, you had better fetter it by
whistling, but in a subdued key. Whenever you
feel like progressing a little farther towards bed, progress. Unfasten your suspenders, take off your
trousers, and fold them so that the first suspender
button on one side shall come against the first suspender button on the other side. In this condition
carry them carefully into your bedroom, and place
them flat between the mattress and the springs of
the bed. It is satisfying to feel that even when
you are asleep you are doing something.

Returning into your dressing-room, pull off your
shirt, after which, in the clothes that remain to you,
dash back into the chilly bedroom and hastily perform your ablutions. Then snatch your dressing-
gown in one hand and your night-gown, or, if you
are fortunate, your pajamas, in the other, step back
into your dressing-room, and huddle yourself around
the fire.

Do not be in any hurry to proceed. The advice
is gratuitous, for it is not likely that you will be.
While you are feeling the delicious, tickling warmth,
dwell on the pleasure that is in store for you. It
seems to me a great pity that people do not do this
more. You can enjoy sleep only by anticipation;
when you are enjoying it, you don't know it; and
when you wake up the next morning, you feel only
regret that it is all over.

When you have become warm through and
through, and when your flesh is beginning to tingle
with the heat, it is time to proceed. After dispos-
ing of the last remnant of the garb that associates

you with the weary day, and after robing yourself in your peaceful night-gown or more æsthetic pajamas, thrust your feet into a pair of soft felt slippers, envelop your body in your fluffy dressing-gown, and bound upon your billowy divan. Then read. It is important that you read the proper things. Not novels. Novels are the sworn enemy of bed; they may drive away the brooding sleepiness, but they are liable to defer indefinitely the blissful joy of sleep. What you should read should be heavy, uninteresting, and adapted to increasing your sleepiness. Personally, I prefer Newman's "Apologia"; but in this matter, latitude may be allowed for individual taste. Ten minutes is as long as you should read, and if you choose the right kind of book, it will be as long as you can read. Moreover, if you have chosen the right kind of book, it will have prepared you for the ensuing devotional mood, which undoubtedly accompanies everybody's bed-going.

After that is all over, clear the long rockers out of the path from the gas fixture to the bedroom door, turn out the light, and go to bed in the form of a ball. When the edge has been taken off the cold, so that you no longer feel like a corpse in its shroud, straighten yourself out gradually, close your eyes, and think slowly and in succession of

> "A flock of sheep that leisurely pass by
> One after one; the sound of rain, and bees
> Murmuring; the fall of rivers, winds and seas,
> Smooth fields, white sheets of water, and—"

You ought to be asleep by that time.

Arthur S. Pier, '95.

THE WRONG SCENT.

THE TRUE STORY OF A "MAUVAIS QUART D'HEURE."

A COLD shiver passed through the manly frame of Mr. Richard Randolph as he stood before an open box lying upon his centre-table and gazed with perturbed countenance at its contents. The hour was late; that is, it was about a quarter after six, which does not leave much time to spare when one is due at a dinner at seven, and must dress and get into Boston from Cambridge within the hour. But it was not lack of leisure that disturbed our friend; in fact, he claimed on ordinary occasions to be able after long practice to perform his toilet and array himself in evening dress in the ridiculously short space of seven minutes; it was not lack of time, I repeat; it was something infinitely worse.

A short retrospection upon our part will be necessary in order fully to understand the situation. Lying upon his writing table was an invitation from a certain society leader of Boston, asking him to dinner upon this very evening, to meet a young and attractive damsel from Baltimore who happened to be visiting her. Richard had of course joyfully accepted, and then as carefully dismissed the whole thing from his mind with his usual nonchalance, only remembering his engagement a few moments before our story opens.

"It's lucky I happened to remember that dinner!" he remarked mentally as he endeavored to find his dress suit. "Mrs. Tyler would have black-listed me!" After a fruitless search in his chiffonier, which failed to reveal any signs of the aforesaid wedding garments, Mr. Randolph realized with a sinking heart that this being his first appearance in society for the season, since it was early in the autumn, his evening clothes were still carefully done up and put away in a box at the top of his closet. "They'll be ruinously creased! I should have sent them to the tailor's ages ago!" he ejaculated as he hastily carried the box out into his study and untied it. Then, as he removed the cover, his courage departed from him. There lay his poor dress suit, creased and crumpled, but that was not all; a strange and noisome odor rose from the box and filled the air,— an odor hated of all men,— a perfume like the mingling of checkerberry, kerosene, and Charles-River-flats-at-low-tide,— the odor of those inventions of Satan that women put in men's clothes to keep out the moths. The smell floated calmly up and tickled the nostrils of our wretched hero; it pervaded the room, hung about his head, and infected his person. He was paralyzed with horror. He remembered how in the spring he had told the "goody" to put away his dress clothes for him, and he now perceived with what thoroughness she had performed her work. Her very words on that occasion returned to his mind: "Dar now, Marse Randolph, Ise done fixed yo' clo's so dey ain't no kind ob insec' can tech 'em. Ise put in some ob my 'moth-balls'!" And he recollected that he had *thanked* her for her thoughtfulness.

He looked at his watch and found that it was just a quarter after six. At first he thought of giving the whole thing up and feigning sudden sickness;

then he remembered the Baltimore girl, and resolved to go at all hazards. First, he subjected the clothes to a vigorous beating; then he hung them out of the window and let the autumn breezes fan them while he got ready to put them on. Nevertheless, after he had dressed, the clothes seemed as odoriferous as ever; the smell was absolutely fiendish. In desperation, he seized an atomizer and deluged himself with vaporized cologne; but, strange to say, this seemed to have no effect,— in fact, if anything, it appeared to put an edge on the already sufficiently penetrating perfume.

All the way into Boston he stood on the front platform with his coat off and tried to air himself, and as he felt the wind whistling through his coat-tails, while the car buzzed over Harvard Bridge, he began to feel more at ease. He thought of the beautiful girl from Baltimore, and reflected that he had been in worse predicaments than this before, and lived through them.

Randolph arrived in good time, and was introduced to the damsel for whom the dinner was given, and then followed a tête-à-tête, during which he shuddered and tried to look pleasant by turns. To his excited imagination the room seemed already full of the odor of "moth-balls," and he awaited with feverish anxiety the moment when it should be discovered by the rest of the company. He did not have long to wait. Mrs. Tyler shortly betrayed signs of nervousness.

"I wonder what is the matter with that lamp!" she exclaimed, glancing at a tall piano-lamp in the corner. Dick was on the *qui vive* in an instant.

"Let me fix it!" he suggested, endeavoring to get as near it as possible. The lamp proved to be in a fairly normal condition, however, and Mrs. Tyler apologized for the unpleasant odor, saying that the lamps were always getting out of order. Dick meanwhile mentally hugged himself and tried to turn the conversation.

The host, who was a trifle late, now entered, and after greeting his guests, turned to his wife with, " Er, Mary, what is this peculiar odor? Is there anything the matter with that lamp? Pray have it fixed as soon as possible."

During the confusion of going out to dinner, Richard congratulated himself upon his escape, yet quaked with apprehension at the thought of what later tortures he might have to endure. His uneasiness was not diminished when he found himself placed beside the girl from Baltimore.

There was a good deal of conversation at first, and our hero flattered himself that perhaps his trials were over, but the hope was in vain. A curious and peculiarly searching perfume began to make itself evident most unmistakably. Dick fairly perspired with agitation, being, as he was, absolutely helpless. He wished the house would catch fire, but this was improbable. The girl from Baltimore was seized with a fit of coughing, which did not improve matters. The hostess beckoned to the butler, who carefully examined all the gas-jets and then shook his head dolefully at her from the pantry door. The guests moved a trifle uneasily. Conversation languished. The servant who passed Dick the soup turned away and stifled a cough.

Someone started to tell an anecdote about General Grant and forgot what he was going to say, when he had reached his description of how "the General sniffed the powder-laden air," and stopped in a plainly embarrassed manner.

Presently there came a dead silence. Dick was racking his brains for a pretext to excuse himself, and had resolved to have an epileptic fit if something did not happen within two minutes. Fortunately or unfortunately, something did happen. He was seized with an uncontrollable desire to sneeze. He felt it coming, and whipped out his handkerchief in time to save himself, but to his horror found that three little white balls had flown from his pocket at the same time, and were now rolling and bouncing about the table, to the amusement of the startled company. For a moment there was silence, then followed an hilarious burst of laughter. Dick, seeing that all was over, laughed confusedly with the others, and resolving to throw himself upon the mercy of his hostess, got up and told the whole story of his sufferings and begged to be forgiven. His account of the matter was received with much mirth, and he was granted complete and final absolution by all present.

"But Mr. Randolph must write this up into a story," cried someone.

"Yes, yes!" resounded on all sides.

"But what shall I call it?" gasped Dick.

"Call it," murmured the girl from Baltimore, glancing slyly at our hero, "call it 'The Wrong Scent.'"

Arthur Cheney Train, '96·

CPSIA information can be obtained
at www.ICGtesting.com
Printed in the USA
BVHW041034310119
539143BV00007B/46/P

9 780267 006649